'Some things never go away,' Alex added bitterly. 'You just have to learn to live with them forever.'

'That's very comforting,' Jennie said sarcastically. 'Please explain to me how I'm going to live with the knowledge that no man will ever want me.'

'Damn it, Jennie!' he ground out, turning on her angrily. 'What makes you think no man will ever want you? If nothing else, Mark Doyle's behaviour tonight should have proved to you that you're a desirable young woman.'

'Oh, sure,' she sneered. 'A minute ago you were warning me off men like Mark and their one-night stands.'

'You want a one-night stand, Jennie? OK, I'm a man. I'll give it to you.'

Books you will enjoy
by ROSEMARY HAMMOND

GAME PLAN

It was said that Jake Donovan had an infallible plan, that would make the women fall at his feet. But, when it didn't work with reserved Claire Talbot, he found to his surprise that he couldn't forget her. . .

FACE VALUE

Christine had agreed to take on one last modelling job before she changed careers entirely. But the stockbroker John Falconer had devised the offer of a commercial for his company simply to meet Chris and offer her another proposition. . .

MY DESTINY

When detective Stephen Ryan made it clear that he wanted to see more of her, Joanna couldn't help but remember the last man she'd loved. Three years ago she had been married to Ross, also a policeman, and he'd died in the line of duty. Couldn't the same happen to Stephen?

THE ONLY MAN

BY

ROSEMARY HAMMOND

MILLS & BOON LIMITED
ETON HOUSE   18–24 PARADISE ROAD
RICHMOND   SURREY   TW9 1SR

First published in Great Britain 1990
by Mills & Boon Limited

© Rosemary Hammond 1990

Australian copyright 1990
Philippine copyright 1990
This edition 1990

ISBN 0 263 76577 6

Set in 10 on 11½ pt Linotron Times
05-9002-50119
Typeset in Great Britain by Centracet, Cambridge
Made and printed in Great Britain

CHAPTER ONE

THE sun was just going down as Jennie stumbled into the house. She closed the front door quietly behind her and started down the hall towards the stairs, moving stealthily past the open door of her father's study, praying the two men inside wouldn't notice her.

'Jennie?' came her father's voice. 'Is that you?'

She stopped short and closed her eyes, still trembling. Then, 'Yes, Dad,' she called in her brightest, most cheerful tone.

She started to walk on, but he called to her again. 'What happened to Peter? I thought you and he were going down to the new house to check on the locks.'

She went to the door and poked her head inside. Her father and his friend, Alex Knight, were sitting in their usual chairs in front of the bay window that overlooked the side garden, already embarked on their weekly game, the chess-board set on a table between then. At the familiar, comfortable sight, her father's medical books lining the walls, her dead mother's photograph on his desk, the roses blooming outside the window in the fading light, the hot tears smarted behind Jennie's eyes.

Forcing them back, she put on a weak smile. 'Peter couldn't stay.' She searched her mind for a plausible lie. 'He had to get back to the hospital tonight.'

Her father snorted. 'That's heck of a way to treat a young intern!' he exclaimed. 'Seems to me they work young doctors a lot harder than they used to.'

He looked across the table at his friend, as though seeking corroboration. Jennie breathed an agonised inward sigh of resignation. As anxious as she was to get away, courtesy demanded that she at least acknowledge the other man's presence.

'Hello, Alex,' she said, giving him a brief nod.

'Jennie,' he said quietly. He leaned back in his chair and gave her a narrow-eyed, searching look. 'Are you all right?'

She put a hand to her throat. 'Of course I'm all right. Why do you ask?'

He shook his head. 'No reason.'

'Well,' she said, 'I'll say goodnight now. I have some things to do upstairs. Have a good game, you two.'

She edged her way out of the room, and once she was safely out of their sight she ran quickly and softly up the stairs until she came to her own bedroom. Flinging the door open, she went inside, closed it behind her, threw herself down on top of the bed and at last gave way to the torrent of grief-stricken tears she'd been bottling up for the past terrible hour.

Finally, exhausted, she slept, and when she opened her eyes again the room was dark. As consciousness returned, the awful scene with Peter came with it. She lay back on the pillow with a groan as the ugly details streamed back into her mind and the whole sickening scenario was replayed once again.

As soon as he'd arrived earlier that evening, she'd known that he had something on his mind, but the awful truth didn't occur to her until they went out into the garden and he suddenly blurted it out. He didn't want to marry her. Their engagement was off. He'd fallen in love with someone else.

She stood at the garden gate staring blankly at him. If she'd been suddenly struck by lightning or pierced by a bullet, she couldn't have been more stunned. Even though she understood his words, her mind could not grasp the fact that this terrible thing was really happening to her.

'I'm sorry, Jen,' he said for the tenth time. 'I didn't want this to happen. I certainly didn't go looking for it.' Pale and shaken, he spread his arms wide in a gesture of defeat. 'I hate like hell to hurt you like this.'

Still paralysed by shock, Jennie continued to stare at him. He'd been running his hands nervously through his straight fair hair while he talked, until now it was standing up on end in short spikes all over his head. He suddenly looked so comical! And a bubble of hysterical laughter grew deep inside her. At the same time hot tears threatened, and she knew that she was close to the edge.

While she fought down the impulse to scream, to laugh, to cry, Peter continued droning on in the same flat, miserable voice, explaining again why he was not coming back to Santa Lucia to enter her father's medical practice after his internship was over in the autumn, as they'd planned, why he'd accepted a residency at the hospital in San Francisco, and why they couldn't get married.

While she listened the shock gradually wore off, and the meaning of his feeble explanations finally penetrated her dulled senses. Her pounding heart settled into a more normal rhythm, and a slow anger began to build deep inside her.

He had been staring down at the ground, kicking nervously at a tuft of grass, waiting for her to speak. It was early evening then, the hot summer sun just lowering in the western sky, the air still close and warm.

He raised his eyes and held out a hand to her in mute appeal. 'Jen——' he began.

She took a step back from him and fixed him with a look of icy calm. 'And so it was all a lie,' she said in a dead, even tone. 'All the plans we made, the house, the furniture, the partnership with my father. All the time you were engaged to me, you were falling in love with someone else.' She laughed harshly. 'I just ordered the wedding invitations yesterday——!'

She could hear her voice rising in hysteria, see the look of alarm on Peter's stricken face. She broke off and turned away from him, biting her lip, fighting back the tears.

'It wasn't like that, Jen,' Peter said, and started once again to explain just how he had been chosen for the coveted residency, how the fact that he and the chief of staff's daughter had fallen in love had nothing to do with it, but by then she didn't even hear him.

On a sudden impulse, she held out her hand and gazed at the diamond solitaire on her ring finger. A shaft of the dying sun had caught its facets, and it sparkled in the brilliant rays. She pulled it off slowly and held it out to him.

'Here,' she said. 'You'll be needing this.'

She turned then, and walked away from him towards the house. He didn't make a move to come after her, nor utter a sound. By the time she reached the wooden porch, she had heard his car door slam, the motor fire, and he had driven off.

She got up off the bed and stumbled into the adjoining bathroom. When she switched on the light she was looking into the mirror, which was directly in front of her. She blinked in the glare and studied her reflection, the short dark hair tousled and untidy, the regular features twisted into a grimace of pain, her normally fair skin red and blotched with tears.

She turned on the cold water and splashed her face, then dried it and looked into the mirror again, making a wry face. It wasn't much improvement. She had never been a great beauty, and her recent fit of crying made her look downright ugly. I *am* ugly, she thought. What did she have to offer a rising young doctor like Peter Fleming?

Why shouldn't he fall in love with someone else? A glamorous blonde, most likely. And one with a real figure. She glanced down at her own slim, almost boyish form, the small, firm breasts virtually non-existent under her stiff cotton shirt, the waist and hips lean, the stomach flat. Hardly a sex symbol to set a man on fire or arouse his lust!

She turned off the bathroom light and walked over to the window. Outside, a full moon was gleaming in the dark night sky, casting its pale glow over the roses blooming there. Every bone and muscle in her body throbbed with a dull, aching pain, her entire being full of gloom.

My life is over, she thought. Everything I ever wanted is gone, the man I loved—still love, in spite of everything—the home we worked for so hard and saved for for so long, the children I'll never have. I might as well be dead.

Suddenly the porch light went on, the front door opened, and the sound of voices drifted out into the night. Looking down, she saw her father and Alex. She couldn't make out what they were saying, but she could see them clearly, probably discussing their chess game, which Alex invariably won. They seemed so comfortable with each other, so normal.

They said goodnight, and after her father went inside Alex stood on the porch for a moment, his arms folded across his chest, looking out into the darkness. Then he reached in his pocket and took out a pipe, filled it, and she could see the pale wreath of smoke wafting on the night breeze as he lit it.

He stepped off the porch and started walking down the path, his tall, straight figure silhouetted against the moonlight. Then he stopped suddenly and turned around, his gaze moving upwards until he seemed to be staring directly at her. Even though she knew that with her lights off he couldn't see her, she moved back abruptly, away from the window.

He'd known something was wrong. She'd fooled her father, at least for the time being, but nothing much escaped Alex Knight. A quiet man, with steady, penetrating grey eyes, she'd always been just a little uneasy around him. Somehow, from the way he looked at her occasionally, he seemed to be able to read her mind, to fathom the deepest secrets of the heart.

This was one secret she was not going to share with anyone, not for a while, not until she came to terms with it herself and decided what in the world she was going to do with the rest of her life.

The next day, Jennie walked down the familiar streets of Santa Lucia on her way to her father's office. The small town looked the same, the June sun already heating up the air, the pavement warm under her feet, even at nine o'clock in the morning.

She spoke to the same people she usually met on her

way to work; the shopkeepers rolling down their striped canvas awnings against the glare of the sun; one of the local lawyers unlocking his office door; the postmistress turning the 'Closed' sign around to read 'Open'.

But it wasn't the same. Yesterday, in the space of one short half-hour, Jennie's whole world had become totally transformed, and she was still reeling from the impact of the blow. Instead of the streets of Santa Lucia, she could have been walking on Mars.

She'd awakened early that morning, at first light, but had purposely stayed in bed, the covers over her head, until she'd heard her father getting ready to leave for his early morning rounds at the tiny local hospital. Peter's brutal rejection was still too raw. She couldn't face anyone else with it, not even her father, until she'd somehow come to terms with it herself.

'Hey, sleeping beauty,' he'd called up to her from the bottom of the stairs. 'You'd better rise and shine if you want a ride to the office.'

'You go ahead, Dad,' she'd called back. 'I'll walk to work.'

The office was on a quiet side-street, a small frame-cottage that her father shared with the local paediatrician. Jennie served as receptionist and assistant for both doctors, and, although she'd had no formal nurse's training, her father and old Dr Watkins had taught her all that she needed to know for their small practices.

The building was shaded by an enormous old acacia tree, and in the summer its fuzzy, fragrant yellow

blossoms covered the narrow flagstone path. Ordinarily, Jennie would have stopped for a while to savour
the sweet scent, pinch off the dead blossoms in the tiny
flower-bed and set the sprinkler running on the patch
of grass beneath the tree, but this morning her head
was filled with a great dark cloud of misery that blotted
out her normal senses, and she merely moved unseeing,
unthinking, up the path.

The first thing she saw when she opened the door
was the photograph of Peter sitting on her desk. She
stood in the doorway staring blankly at it, remembering
once again in a sudden painful rush the years they had
spent together, the plans they had made, the house all
ready for them to move in, the wedding only two weeks
away, and the tears of self-pity began to flow.

Fighting for control, she stumbled over the threshold
and slammed the door behind her. Still sobbing, she
went directly to the desk and threw the photograph
into the waste-paper basket. She gripped the back of
her chair and took in a deep breath of the close, still
air. As she inhaled the familiar, pungent, antiseptic
odour, she had a sudden fleeting vision of the drugs
cupboard, kept under lock and key, full of potentially
lethal narcotics.

For one second she was tempted. Although her
father carried the only key with him at all times, it
would be a simple matter to break into it, take out a
handful of the most powerful pills, swallow them down
and just give up.

Today was Thursday, her father's morning at the
hospital's outpatient clinic. He wouldn't come to the
office until after lunch. By then it would be too late.
What did it matter? She felt dead already, anyway.

Then her eye fell on the appointment book on her

desk, the list of instructions written out beside it in her father's near-illegible hand, the dosages for injections, orders for blood tests, prescriptions to be distributed, all carefully spelled out so that she could handle the morning's patients on her own.

With a deep sigh, she reached for a tissue, dried her eyes, blew her nose and shoved her handbag in the bottom drawer of the desk. Even if it was tempting to lose her own life, she had no right to put the health of others in jeopardy.

Somehow Jennie managed to get through the day without breaking down again, but by evening she knew that she would have to tell her father what had happened. He'd given her puzzled looks on the drive home when she'd responded in monosyllables to his attempts at conversation, and he couldn't miss the way she'd merely picked at her dinner.

In fact, the whole world would soon know about it, since all her careful plans would have to be cancelled as soon as possible, and she would need his help to face that.

After clearing the table and serving their after-dinner coffee, she sat back down at the kitchen table, still debating how to tell him, while he lit the one cigar of the day he allowed himself. Then, blowing out a wreath of smoke, he gave her a thoughtful look.

'All right, Jennie,' he said. 'What's up?'

Willing herself not to break down, she forced out a crooked smile and said, 'Well, Dad. I've been jilted.'

His eyes flew open, then narrowed angrily. 'What? Are you serious?'

She nodded glumly. 'Afraid so.'

'Do you mean to tell me,' he sputtered, 'that Peter. . .' He waved a hand in the air, unable to go on.

'Right,' she said with another nod. 'He's accepted a residency at the hospital in San Francisco. He's not coming back to Santa Lucia when his internship is over. He's not going into practice with you. And he's not going to marry me.' She took a deep breath. 'In fact, Peter has fallen in love.'

'Fallen in love?' her father repeated in a shocked tone. Then he snorted noisily. 'Peter's been in love with you since you were children. What do you mean, fallen in love?'

She shrugged her shoulders wearily. 'I guess these things just happen. Who knows why? I've been trying to figure it out myself, and I think it was probably mostly habit with Peter and me.' She sighed. 'And you'll have to admit, I'm no raving beauty. Now he's found someone who really attracts him. I guess you can't blame him for that, Dad.'

'Can't blame him?' he shouted. 'I damn well do blame him. And what about the practice? Isn't he even man enough to come to me himself and tell me he's changed his mind about that? The plans were all made. What am I supposed to do now?'

Jennie had to smile. In typical male fashion, once the initial shock had passed, he was far more concerned and indignant about his practice than he was about his daughter's broken heart.

As though able to read her thoughts, he waved his cigar in the air and gave her a sheepish look. 'I mean to say, Jennie, that you're young, an attractive, intelligent, capable girl. Someone else will come along for you, someone much better than Peter Fleming! But where,' he added plaintively, 'where will I find another bright young doctor willing to bury himself in a hick town like Santa Lucia?'

Just then the front doorbell rang. Her father shoved his chair back and jumped to his feet, obviously relieved at the interruption. 'I'll get that,' he said. 'It'll be Alex. We didn't finish our game last night and he said he'd be over after supper.'

When he had gone, Jennie got up to rinse out their cups and put on another pot of coffee for her father and his friend. As she stood at the sink, she could hear the front door open, and her father's loud, indignant voice shouting, 'Alex, you won't believe what Jennie just told me,' and she cringed inwardly, the hot blood of shame rushing up into her face.

Methodically, woodenly, she continued to measure out the coffee. As she put on the pot to drip and finished straightening up the kitchen, her one thought was to flee to the safety of her own room where she wouldn't have to face her father or Alex Knight or anyone else. But when she had finally finished her chores and turned to leave, she saw Alex standing in the doorway watching her.

'Hello, Alex,' she said, giving him a bright smile. She dried her hands and hung the towel neatly on the rack under the counter. 'The coffee will be ready in a few minutes. Are you and Dad going to finish your famous chess game tonight?' She started walking briskly towards the door. 'Honestly, I don't see how you two have the patience to sit there week after week——'

'Jennie,' he broke in, his voice low, but quite firm.

She had reached him by now, but he stood there solidly in the doorway, blocking her exit. She glanced up at him, and the look of grave concern on his lean face startled her, so she dropped her eyes and stared down at the floor to cover her confusion.

'Jennie,' he said again in a softer tone, 'your father told me what happened with Peter. I know it's none of my business, but I've known you since you were only sixteen, after all, and I think that gives me some privileges.' He smiled down at her. 'Anyway,' he went on, 'I just wanted to tell you how truly sorry I am. And what a damn fool I think Peter Fleming is to let you get away from him.'

She raised her eyes and stared at him in disbelief. In all the years she'd known him, it was probably the longest speech—and certainly the most personal—he'd ever made to her. Ordinarily the mildest of men, rather silent and withdrawn, merely a friend of her father's, it had never occurred to her that she even existed as a real person in his mind.

'Thanks, Alex,' she said shortly. 'But if it was going to happen, I suppose it's best to get it over with now.'

'Is there anything I can do?' he asked quietly.

Once again he'd taken her by surprise. He'd never shown the slightest interest in her or her feelings in the past, and she didn't want his pity now.

'No,' she said. 'There's nothing anyone can do.'

She heard her voice waver and felt the hot tears gather behind her eyes once again. Soon they would spill over. Sympathy always did that to her, and she began to grow resentful towards Alex for intruding on her grief, as well as towards her father for telling him she'd been jilted in the first place.

He searched her face carefully for a few seconds, raised a hand as though to reach out for her, but when she immediately went rigid and drew away from him he dropped it at his side again, then silently stood aside and let her pass.

As she slowly mounted the stairs to her room, she had the uneasy feeling that the tall man was staring after her. Then she heard her father call to him, and when she turned around to see him walk off down the hall towards the study, she raced up the remaining stairs, rushed into her bedroom and closed the door.

Leaning back against it, she closed her eyes and let the tears fall. If only this awful feeling of desolation would pass! she agonised to herself. People always said that only time healed sorrow, but how long would it take to get over it? It was Jennie's first real experience with genuine grief. Her mother had died when she was only two years old, too young to feel the impact of that great loss.

She went into the bathroom to throw cold water on her face, and just as she was drying it off the telephone by the side of her bed began to ring. She didn't want to talk to anybody, but she knew that her father wouldn't answer while he and Alex were so immersed in their game, and they had a long-standing agreement that she would take any calls, in case of an emergency with one of his patients.

She went into the bedroom and lifted the receiver. 'Dr Corbett's residence,' she said.

'Jennie? It's Peggy.'

'Oh. Hi, Peggy.'

'Is it true?'

Jennie groaned inwardly. News travelled with the speed of light in Santa Lucia, but she hadn't dreamt that it would have spread quite this fast. Could she hedge? Pretend she didn't know what Peggy was talking about? No, not Peggy! Nothing escaped her.

'Yes, Peggy,' she said at last. 'It's true.'

She and Peggy had been friends since first grade. They were as different as night and day, a fact which only seemed to cement their friendship more solidly as the years passed. While Peggy was firmly embarked on a career as a buyer for a local department store, all Jennie had ever wanted to do was marry Peter and make a home.

'Well, that rat!' Peggy breathed indignantly. 'Why didn't you tell me about it?'

'It only happened last night,' Jennie replied stiffly. 'Just how did you find out so soon?'

'Oh, you know how word gets around,' Peggy said airily. 'His mother told her sister-in-law, who is my boss's cousin. Something like that, anyway.'

'Peggy,' Jennie said, horrified, 'you don't suppose it'll get printed in the local paper?'

Peggy laughed. 'Of course not. It's hardly earth-shaking news. To tell you the truth, I was delighted when I heard about it. Now that you're rid of that macho wimp, maybe you can get on with more important things.'

In spite of herself, Jennie couldn't suppress a giggle. 'How can a man be macho and a wimp at the same time? And what do you mean by getting on with my life?'

'All macho men are wimps at heart,' Peggy stated firmly. 'They just don't realise it. And what I mean by getting on with your life is that now you can start thinking about using your talents instead of burying yourself as a small-town doctor's wife.'

'Oh, Peggy, please. Not that old song and dance again. We've been over all this before. A career might be fine for you, but you know darned well that all I ever wanted was to marry Peter, have children, make a home——' She broke off as her voice cracked.

'OK, OK,' Peggy said in a softer tone. 'Don't pay any attention to me. I can't help shooting off my mouth. But I'd like to make one of my famous predictions.'

Jennie had to smile. 'And what's that?'

'Only this—that one of these days, and sooner than you think, you're going to thank your stars that this happened.'

'You might be right, Peggy, but I don't feel very grateful at the moment.'

'No, I don't imagine you do, knowing you. I still think you should give serious thought to a career, but if marriage and a home are what you really want, then you'll get them. And it'll be with the right man next time. I never was thrilled about your plans to marry Peter Fleming.'

'Well, at least you don't have that to worry about now,' Jennie commented drily. 'Or probably anyone else, for that matter.'

'What do you mean by that?'

'Oh, I don't know. Peter has been the only man in my life for so long that I can't imagine anyone else ever wanting me.'

'Now don't start that. You know what I think?'

'No, but I'm sure you're going to tell me.'

'I think you were more in love with the idea of getting married, of making your dream come true, than you ever were with Peter. What's more, I'd be willing to bet that what you're really worried about is having to face people, not losing Peter.'

'You couldn't be more wrong,' Jennie said flatly. 'I *loved* Peter.' She sniffled loudly. 'I still do.'

'OK, have it your way,' Peggy said with a sigh. 'How about lunch tomorrow?'

Jennie hesitated. Lunch with Peggy meant a long, painful session of probing into her psyche, and she wasn't sure that she was up to it yet. Still, it had to be faced eventually.

'All right,' she said.

'I'll meet you at one o'clock at Dino's. My treat.'

They hung up then, and, in spite of her annoyance with Peggy's certainties and their fundamental differences in outlook on life, Jennie felt much better after talking to her friend.

She slipped off her shoes, lay back on the bed and closed her eyes. Sorrow was an exhausting process, and she felt limp and drained from fighting it off all day. As she drifted off into a fitful doze, her last thought was of Peter. She wondered if Peggy was right, that it *was* more the loss of habit and of the promise of security, and even the dread of facing people that had hit her so hard, and not losing Peter at all.

They'd been a couple for as long as she could remember. There never was a time in her life that Peter wasn't part of it. How could she go on without that assurance of his presence beside her? How could she. . .

The blessed release of sleep descended before the question had formed in her mind, and when she awoke again it was dark outside and her stomach was growling with hunger. From below came the sound of voices, and her first fuzzy thought was that Peter had come back.

She sat bolt upright, every muscle tense, her ears straining for the sound of his voice. But as her head cleared she realised that it was only Alex leaving. She switched on the lamp beside her bed and glanced at the clock. It was past eleven. No wonder she was starved. She'd hardly eaten anything all day.

When she heard Alex's car drive off she slipped on her shoes and went downstairs. A sandwich from the left-over ham that she'd only picked at earlier and a glass of milk sounded like heaven.

Her father was just coming from the front door as she reached the bottom of the stairs, and he gazed up in surprise when he saw her coming towards him.

'How are you feeling, Jennie?' he asked.

'Better,' she replied. 'I was just going to make myself a snack. Are you hungry?'

'No, but I might have the last of the coffee and an extra cigar to keep you company.'

She gazed at him in some concern. So preoccupied with her own troubles, she'd forgotten all about his precarious state of health. 'Should you, Dad? Dr Samuels said——'

He raised a hand. 'Don't tell me about it,' he said grimly. 'Samuels is a fussy old maid. I'm a doctor. I know what's best for my own health.'

Jennie knew better than to argue with him. The mild heart attack he'd had six months ago had frightened him, but apparently not badly enough to make him give up his tobacco and coffee.

In the kitchen, while she sliced the ham and made up her sandwich, she thought about the brief conversation she'd had with Alex earlier, and once again felt the sting of resentment towards her father for discussing her problem with him.

When she sat down opposite her father, she gave him an accusing look. 'Dad, did you have to tell Alex about me and Peter?'

His tufted grey eyebrows shot up. 'Surely you don't think you can keep it a secret for long in this town?'

'No, but it was embarrassing to have him confront me with it.'

'Alex means well, honey. He was very concerned about you. You know how fond he is of you.'

Jennie stared at him. 'I do? You could have fooled me. He's never paid the slightest attention to me before.' She took a bite of sandwich, chewed thoughtfully, then washed it down with a swallow of milk.

'Well,' her father was saying, 'Alex is a very private man. Doesn't show his feelings much.'

'You've been good friends for a long time,' she commented.

'Seven or eight years now,' he replied. 'Ever since he came to Santa Lucia and bought the old winery. He's really done wonders with it, too. Made it into a paying proposition.'

'Where did he come from?'

Her father shrugged. 'I don't really know. San Francisco, I think. As I said, he's a very private man. He's never told me much about his past, and I've never asked.'

'It sounds as though he might be a very lonely man,' Jennie said thoughtfully.

'Why do you say that?'

'I don't know. Maybe because I'm feeling lonely myself for the first time in my life and can relate to it better.'

Her father gazed at her for several moments, then stubbed out his cigar and drained the last of his coffee. He raised a warning finger in the air and shook it at her. 'Now don't do that, Jennie,' he said. 'Don't start wallowing in self-pity. I know this was a terrible thing for you, but you'll come out of it all right, and I say good riddance to the young fool if he doesn't see what a prize he was getting.'

'Apparently he didn't think so,' she said drily.

'And you mustn't be bitter, either,' he went on in the same warning tone. 'You're so young, Jennie. You have your whole life ahead of you. One of these days some young man will come along who will make you glad this happened. You mark my words.' He got up from the table, yawned and stretched. 'Now, it's bedtime for your old dad. Will you be all right?'

'I'm fine, Dad. Goodnight.'

When he had gone Jennie finished the last of her sandwich and sat at the table sipping her milk. Peggy and her father both meant well, she knew that, and they both wanted what was best for her. But their encouraging words had fallen on deaf ears.

In her heart of hearts, she was convinced that there never would be a man to take Peter's place, nor would she ever have the home, the family, the security that she craved. If Peter didn't want her, why should anyone else?

Suddenly the sandwich that she had downed so ravenously and that had tasted so good turned to acid in her churning stomach. She would never get over this, never! She pushed the plate and glass aside, folded her arms on the table and put her head down. All she could see ahead was blank misery, emptiness, lovelessness, and she didn't think she could bear it.

CHAPTER TWO

To Jennie's amazement, she did live through the next few weeks. By the end of them, she even found that she could meet people on the street and carry on a conversation in a normal tone of voice, rather than slink past them in the hope of not being noticed, or cringe whenever she heard someone call her name.

No one laughed at her or pointed at her, and if they whispered behind her back at least she didn't know about it. The world didn't come to an end, and, although she was still depressed over the sudden crash of all her hopes, and the future still stretched before her in bleak desolation, she began to feel as though she just might be able to get on with some kind of life, after all.

The hardest part had been cancelling the wedding plans—the church, the minister, the flowers, the invitations. Peggy had been an enormous help, taking much of the practical burden off her shoulders. Peter could take care of the house himself.

By now, all those details had been taken care of. It was the first of July, and the whole town was deep into preparations for its annual *fiesta* on the fourth, Independence Day. Colourful crêpe paper banners had been strung from the lamp-posts across Main Street, a bandstand had been set up in front of the city hall, and the makeshift kangaroo court gaolhouse was ready to receive its prisoners.

There would be a parade, a street dance, music,

prize booths, even a gypsy fortune-teller, and as Jennie sat in the office three days before the great event, listening to the high-school marching band limp through a practice session, she wished she could talk herself into a more receptive mood. This year her enthusiasm for the celebration was at its lowest ebb.

With the window open, the off-key band music was so painful to her ears that she could hardly think. It was another hot morning, the sprinklers running on the grass outside, and not a breath of a breeze blowing. Finally, unable to stand the excruciating cacophony as the band marched back and forth on the street in front of the office, she got up to close the window so that she could concentrate.

Just as she reached it the little bell at the top of the front door tinkled, and she turned around to see a tall man with flaming auburn hair step inside.

'Mark!' she said. 'What are you doing here?'

He shut the door behind him and strode jauntily over to the reception desk, a mischievous look on his handsome face. He perched on the edge of the desk, folded his arms across his chest and grinned broadly at her.

'Why, I came to see my favourite girl,' he said. 'Why else?'

Jennie cocked her head to one side and gave him a narrow-eyed look. 'It couldn't be to sell Dad some more of your wonder drugs, could it?'

He raised his hands in the air and his eyes widened in mock horror. 'Heaven forbid I should ever harbour such a crass motive,' he intoned piously. 'However, if Dr Corbett does just happen to be here, I could be persuaded to show him the very latest in antibiotics from our laboratories.'

Jennie shut the window, instantly muffling the racket from outside, then crossed over to her desk and sat down. With a wry smile at Mark, she said, 'Well, you're out of luck. Sorry, but Dad was called out on an emergency.'

Bracing an elbow on the desk-top, he leaned his long body across it and gazed into her eyes. 'I told you I came to see you.'

'Hah!' she snorted.

He straightened up and gave her a hurt look. 'You doubt my intentions?' he asked, laying a hand dramatically on his chest.

Mark Doyle was the local representative for a pharmaceutical company that her father dealt with. Extremely self-confident, aware of his good looks, a snappy dresser, he showed up periodically to tout his wares, and, a brilliant salesman to the core, had carried on a playful flirtation with Jennie ever since she'd first started working for her father.

Jennie spread her hands flat on the top of the desk, and was just about to tell him exactly what she thought of his intentions when his glance flicked downwards, then remained fixed on her bare left hand.

'Hey,' he said in a more serious tone, 'what happened to the sparkler? Out for a good cleaning before the wedding?'

Jennie flushed brick-red. Quickly she withdrew her hands and clasped them tightly in her lap. 'Something like that,' she said, hoping to close the subject.

He continued to gaze dubiously at her, however, and she knew that he didn't quite believe her. He'd have to find out eventually, anyway. She might as well tell him herself.

'It's off,' she said curtly.

'I can see that,' he replied.

'I mean the engagement.'

'Ah,' he said, nodding owlishly, immediately sliding off the desk and backing off a few paces.

It was almost funny, Jennie thought as she watched his expression change from thoughtful to downright wary. Mark had been eager enough to play the ardent suitor when she'd been safely engaged to another man, but now that she was free his first instinct was to withdraw.

For a moment she toyed with the idea of having some fun with him by pretending to take his old teasing flirtatiousness seriously, telling him she could go out with him now. But her heart wasn't in it. Even though she had always known that his interest in her was never serious, it still stung to see how quickly he dropped even the pretence once she was actually available.

This clear evidence of what she already suspected, that she simply held no vestige of appeal for any man, resurrected all the hurt, and the dull ache that she had been fighting off every waking moment of the past two weeks gripped her heart again.

To cover it up, she gave him a bright smile. 'Don't take it so hard, Mark,' she said lightly. Then, dropping her eyes to the chart on her desk, added, 'These things happen, you know.'

'Gosh, I'm really sorry, Jennie,' he stammered awkwardly.

There was a long, tense silence. Jennie sat burning with shame and embarrassment, staring blindly down at the open folder, the words swimming before her eyes. She wished he would just go. He'd made his point. She wasn't interested in Mark Doyle, in any case. He was too cocky, too flamboyant, too insincere.

But, a little voice whispered, it would have been nice to have been asked.

Finally, Mark cleared his throat and edged his way towards the door. 'Well, I guess I'll take off now. Got appointments at the hospital all day. I'll be in town for a few days—wouldn't miss the great *fiesta*, you know. Maybe I can catch your father later.'

'Sure, Mark,' she said, with another tight smile. 'See you later.'

He departed in a flash, the little bell jangling noisily as he virtually slammed the door behind him. Jennie had visions of him running down the path, hellbent on getting out of there before she pinned him down. What did he think I was going to do? she thought disgustedly. Attack him?

She got up and poured herself a cup of coffee, then stood at the window, gazing out at the band parading back and forth, while she drank it. She should try to get into a more festive mood, she thought, at least for her father's sake. He always took the *fiesta* so seriously, even growing a beard for the occasion, as did most of the men in town.

Just then a battered station-wagon pulled up at the kerb, and Alex Knight got out. He stood on the pavement for a moment, tall and lean in his faded jeans, his hands shoved in the back pockets, watching the band with a look of tolerant amusement on his tanned face as they finally gave up and scattered.

Then he turned and started walking up the path. The bell at the door jangled, and he stepped inside.

'Good morning, Alex,' Jennie said.

He nodded. 'Morning, Jennie.'

'If you've come for Dad, I'm afraid he was called away.'

'We did have a lunch date,' he said. 'Any way of telling if he'll be back by noon?'

'Afraid not. You know how those things are.'

He nodded again and glanced at his watch. 'Well, it's almost noon now. If you don't mind, I'll wait here for him for a few minutes. Then, if he doesn't show up, maybe I can talk you into joining me?'

Jennie stared at him. 'Me?'

He laughed shortly. 'Why not? Are you ashamed to be seen in public with an old man like me?'

Old man? She gave him a closer look, watching him as he strolled over to the chair by the window, picked up a magazine, then sat down and leaned back comfortably, his long legs spread before him, leafing through it. How old was he?

As her father's friend, she'd always automatically put him in that generation: late forties, early fifties. But he couldn't possibly be that old. His face was smooth and tanned, and the crinkle of tiny lines around his eyes, the deeper creases from his straight nose to the corners of his mouth, looked as though they had been put there by hard experience rather than age.

He walked like a young man, too, his step quick and athletic, even graceful, and, although there were a few strands of grey in his black hair, she noticed for the first time that it was still thick and glossy, shining brilliantly now where the sun's rays coming in through the window glinted on it.

'Alex,' she said in a thoughtful tone, 'can I ask you a personal question?'

He looked up from the magazine. 'Sure,' he said. 'You can ask.' He smiled broadly, revealing even white teeth. 'If it's too personal, I just won't answer.'

'Fair enough. OK, then, how old are you?'

'I'm thirty-seven,' he replied promptly. 'An old man, as I said. At least from the point of view of twenty-three, I'm sure.'

Somehow thirty-seven didn't seem that old, especially now that she felt she had aged so much herself from her bitter experience. He had turned back to his magazine, but she continued to stare at him, wondering once again what had put those lines on his face.

Just then her father burst inside, harried and perspiring. 'Oh, good,' he said to Alex. 'I'm glad you're here. For a while I was afraid I wasn't going to make our lunch date, but Mrs Cardozo came through on schedule with a nine-pound offspring, and I'm free as the breeze.' He turned to Jennie. 'Anything critical, honey?'

'No. Mark was in, but he said he'd catch you later.'

'Well, that's not important. He just wants to sell me something I don't need. You ready to go, Alex?'

The two men went out together, and Jennie was alone again. As she listened to Alex's station-wagon drive away, she felt oddly disappointed that they hadn't included her—something she never would have dreamed of thinking two weeks ago when she'd been so wrapped up in Peter.

If she hadn't been feeling so sorry for herself, she would have had to laugh. Things had come to a pretty pass when she could feel this let down because she was left out of a luncheon with her father and one of his friends!

On the day of the *fiesta*, the office was closed, as was every other office and shop in Santa Lucia, and Jennie had carefully planned for every hour. In years past, she had looked forward to the annual festivities with eager anticipation, but this year her heart wasn't even in the rest of her *life*, much less a silly party where all the women in town dressed up as Latin *señoritas* and the men tried to look dashing in their new beards and gaucho costumes.

The house needed a good cleaning, her clothes needed laundering, she could wash her hair, do her nails, perhaps even get her father's study organised while he was gone.

He had just left for the hospital that morning, and she was sitting at the kitchen table drinking a last cup of coffee and leafing idly through the morning paper when the telephone on the nearby counter-top rang.

With a frown of annoyance, she hesitated a moment, tempted not to answer it. But the long habit of duty as a doctor's daughter won in the end, and with a sigh she reached over to pick it up.

'Dr Corbett's residence.'

'Hi,' came Peggy's cheerful voice. 'It's me. What time do you want me to pick you up this evening?'

'Pick me up?' Jennie asked, puzzled. 'What for?'

'For the party, of course!' Peggy exclaimed impatiently. 'What do you think?'

'Oh, didn't I tell you? I'm not going.'

'Not going? Are you crazy? We always go to the *fiesta* together. I think it's against the law not to. Come on, now, can you be ready by seven o'clock? The potluck supper starts at eight, and if we get there early we can find a good table. Then when the dance starts at nine——'

'Peggy!' Jennie broke in. 'I told you. I'm not going.'

There was a short silence. Then Peggy went on in a

hurt tone, 'Well, all right, Jennie, if that's the way you want to be.'

'Come on, Peggy. Try to understand. I just don't feel up to it this year.'

'OK. Fine. Stay at home and mope. I don't care. I can always play double solitaire with my grandmother——'

'Oh, Peggy, stop it! You can go without me. I'm lousy company these days, anyway. I'd only spoil it for you.'

'Sure,' Peggy continued airily. 'Don't worry about me. I guess it won't kill me to miss one *fiesta* in my lifetime.'

Jennie ground her back teeth together in frustration. She knew quite well that Peggy was blackmailing her, manipulating her into going, and that if her friend kept it up she'd have to give in eventually. But she refused to go down without a fight.

'I don't have anything to wear,' she said sulkily.

'Oh, I can fix you up there,' Peggy returned brightly. 'I've got tons of outfits to choose from. I'll come over early, around six o'clock, and we can try them on. See you then.'

There was a sharp click in Jennie's ear. Slowly, she hung up the telephone. She braced her elbows on the table, rested her chin in her hands and stared glumly out of the window at the blue blossoms of the jacaranda tree in the garden.

'Outmanoeuvred again,' she muttered to herself. Peggy was an absolute genius at these sparring matches.

She finished the dregs of her coffee, rinsed out her cup at the sink and went upstairs to get dressed. She could still get her chores done. Anything to pass the time.

'No!' Peggy said firmly. 'Definitely not that old black. You'd look like you were going to a funeral. We go with the red satin you've got on. It's perfect with your colouring. Puts a little bloom in those pale cheeks.'

'Are you kidding?' Jennie exploded. 'I look like a Spanish tart!'

'Good,' Peggy stated firmly. 'That's what you're supposed to look like.'

After experimenting all afternoon with costumes from previous years, Jennie had decided on a sedate black dress with a matching lace shawl. It looked festive enough, but the sombre colour mirrored her mood.

Then Peggy had shown up with the old red satin dress, a relic of her slimmer days, unearthed from her overstuffed wardrobes, and had insisted that Jennie at least try it on. The minute she'd seen her reflection in the mirror, she'd known it just wouldn't do.

'This neckline is way too low,' she objected.

'It's supposed to be that way.' Peggy giggled. 'Besides, there's not an awful lot there to expose.'

Jennie gave her a dirty look. 'That's not funny.'

'Oh, don't be so sensitive. You should be glad you're so small-busted. You'll keep your nice firm figure forever.'

'Some figure! My collarbones stick out further than my chest.'

'You're just too thin. How much weight have you lost in the past few weeks, anyway?'

'I don't know. And I don't care. And I'm *not* going to appear in public tonight in this dress.' She reached behind her to unzip the back of the tight dress.

'OK, have it your way. And when Peter sees you wearing that black old lady's dress he'll know exactly how much you've been pining away for him.'

Jennie gave her a sharp look. 'He won't even be there.'

'Oh? He's never missed a *fiesta* before, to my knowledge.'

'Well, there are a lot of things he never did before that don't seem to faze him now.'

Still, Peggy's insinuation had struck a nerve. What if Peter did show up and saw her in the black dress? It did look funereal, and the last thing she wanted was for him to have the slightest clue as to how she'd been grieving for him. Besides, she was getting over it. She was sleeping better, food didn't turn her stomach the way it used to, and the future didn't look quite as dismal as it had at first.

She took another look in her bedroom mirror. If her figure had been more voluptuous, like Peggy's, she couldn't possibly have worn the revealing red dress with its low, round neckline, tightly cinched waist and flaring, ruffled skirt. But, slim as she was, she could probably get away with it without looking too blatantly seductive.

'Oh, all right,' she grumbled. 'I'll wear the darned thing. No one's going to notice me, anyway.'

Peggy raised her eyes heavenward. 'As your oldest friend, my dear, let me be blunt and tell you that I'm getting a little sick of your self-pity.'

Stung, Jennie turned on her. 'That's all right for you to say, *friend*! You've never been jilted.'

'Oh, phooey on jilted. Peter was never right for you, and you know it. He's a small man with big ambitions.

You can do lots better than Peter Fleming, and frankly I was delighted when the marriage was called off.'

Jennie retreated into silence. Peggy had always been the popular, sought-after one. With her outgoing personality and full, rounded figure, she'd had her pick of boys from the time they'd both started dating, and had already broken two engagements, while Peter was the only one who'd ever seemed remotely interested in Jennie herself. She'd counted on that lasting forever, and at the painful reminder the tears threatened again.

She closed her eyes tightly, blinking the tears back, then glanced over at Peggy, who was still sitting on the bed, watching her carefully. With a proud lift of her chin, she gathered up the full red skirt in a wide sweep and flounced past Peggy, picking up the white lace shawl from the bed as she went. When she reached the door, she turned round to face her friend.

'Well, come on, Peggy. If we're going to the *fiesta*, we'd better be on our way.'

Everything about the *fiesta* was so familiar to Jennie that by the time they got there she had forgotten her earlier reluctance and was actually looking forward to the traditional celebration that honoured California's long Spanish heritage.

It was always the same, year after year, for as long as she could remember, the same sights, smells, sounds, the very feel of the balmy night air. One full block of Main Street had been cordoned off for a street dance, and the pavements were lined with tents and booths. The area was brightly lit, with throngs of people milling about, all in brightly coloured Spanish costume of one sort or another.

Peggy had to park her car two blocks away and, as

the two girls walked along, the sweet-scented, spreading acacia trees overhead mingled with the delicious aromas of hot buttered popcorn and spicy Mexican food. The closer they came, the louder the dance-band blared in their ears, competing with the shouts and laughter of the crowd.

They made their way through the crowd to the supper tent, which was decorated with red, white and blue paper streamers. It was stifling inside under the heavy canvas, and Peggy immediately made for the bar.

'You stand in the food queue,' she said to Jennie. 'I'll get us something cold to drink. Beer OK for you?'

Jennie nodded. 'Sounds good.'

She got in line, and in a few minutes Peggy came back with two ice-cold mugs of foaming beer. Jennie took a long, grateful swallow that immediately went to her head. As the queue inched forward she continued to sip at the beer, listening with half an ear to Peggy's running commentary on the townspeople gathered around them.

'Honestly,' she was saying loudly in Jennie's ear, 'you'd think this town could come up with some interesting new men once a year, at least. Look at them!'

Jennie followed her friend's gaze, and had to admit that she agreed with her. Most of the eligible men of their generation had either married young and settled into a family business, or left Santa Lucia right out of school for greener pastures in San Francisco or Los Angeles, which offered far more lucrative career opportunities.

'Oh, look,' Peggy said, pointing as they lurched ahead another six inches. 'There, over in the corner.

It's your father and Alex Knight.' She turned to Jennie. 'Now, there's an interesting man!'

Jennie goggled at her. 'My father?'

'No, silly. Alex. He looks quite dashing tonight, with his black beard and flowing white shirt.'

Jennie searched the crowd and finally spotted the two men. They were some distance away, standing by a crowded table, holding their plates in one hand and beer mugs in the other. As her eye fell on them, she noticed that Alex was staring fixedly at her, a bemused expression on his lean, tanned face.

He raised one hand in a brief greeting, then turned to her father, who immediately waved, beckoning them forward.

Peggy nudged her from behind. 'Why don't you go on over and get them to save us some seats at the table? I'll get the food. What do you want?'

'Oh, I don't know. Whatever you're having.' She hesitated. 'Why don't you go yourself, and I'll stay in line?'

'Why?'

Jennie shrugged. 'Well, you're the one who thinks Alex is dashing.'

The truth was that she was a little hesitant about facing him or her father in the revealing red costume. From the moment they had stepped into the brightly lit, crowded tent she had begun to regret letting Peggy talk her into it. Not only did she feel totally exposed by the low, sweeping neckline, but the cheap, sleazy material had fast started to wilt in the dust and heat, and was now clinging damply to her bare skin.

'Oh, go on,' Peggy urged, giving her a little shove. 'Besides, he looks taken. Get a load of Betty Furlong hanging all over him.'

Obediently, Jennie started to pick her way around the tables towards her father's corner. The two men had sat down on the bench, and as she came nearer she saw with amusement that Peggy was right. Betty Furlong was a nurse at the hospital, a thirtyish, buxom blonde divorcee, who was sitting so close to Alex by now that she was almost in his lap.

'Hi, Dad,' she said, coming up to the table. 'Betty.' She glanced at Alex. 'That's a lovely beard, Alex.' It was, too: thick, black, well-trimmed, it gave him a lean, satanic look that was almost menacing.

'I'm glad you like it,' he said, stroking it and edging away from Betty. 'But I only grew it to stay out of gaol. It comes off tomorrow.' He gave her a swift, appraising glance. 'That's quite a costume you have on, young lady.'

Just then, Betty, who had obviously had more than her share of whatever it was that she was drinking, knocked over the pitcher of beer in the middle of the table, and it immediately flowed towards Alex, dripping into his lap.

'Oh, Alex!' Betty cried. 'I'm sorry. Here, let me help you mop it up.'

She leaned over him, clinging to him and dabbing ineffectually at his clothing, while Alex, frowning, tried to edge away from her.

'That's all right, Betty,' he said firmly, holding her by the wrist. 'I can manage, if you'll just let me get up.'

'Oh, but it's my fault,' she slurred, and grabbed the opening of his loose shirt with her other hand.

Alex continued to back away, and there was a sudden sound of tearing material as the front of the thin shirt ripped away at the shoulder seam. Alex quickly grabbed at the loose sleeve, holding the two pieces together, but not until Jennie had seen the long, livid scar that slashed from his right shoulder down across his chest.

Betty Furlong was sobbing loudly and apologising drunkenly through her tears at the same time, while Alex sat there, rigid as a stone statue, his grey eyes blazing, his face brick-red, clutching his torn shirt, and obviously making a superhuman effort to stay calm.

'It's all right, Betty,' he said finally in a cold, even tone. He lifted his long legs up over the bench and rose to his feet. 'I'll have to go home and change,' he said to Jennie's father. 'Do you want to come with me, Jim?'

Dr Corbett got up. 'No. I guess not.' He stretched widely. 'I've had about all the *fiesta* I can take for one year. Think I'll go home and go to bed.'

Jennie was just about to say that she would go with him when Peggy came up to the table with two steaming plates of tacos, enchiladas and tamales piled high. She raised them triumphantly in the air.

'Success at last!' she cried.

Then her smile faded as Betty, still sniffling audibly into her handkerchief, her mascara running down her face, leaped up from the table and ran off; Alex, stone-faced and still clutching his shirt, nodded briefly at her, then stalked away in the opposite direction, with Dr Corbett close behind him.

Jennie stood staring after the two men, still dazed by the sight of Alex's scar. No wonder, she thought, that on the hottest summer days, when all the other men in town either wore their shirts unbuttoned, or stripped down to T-shirts, or even went around bare-chested, Alex's chest and shoulders were always covered.

What could have happened? Was that the reason for

the distance he seemed to put between himself and everyone else in town? Her father was his only real friend, and her father was a doctor. He was polite to everyone, even friendly, in a remote kind of way, but if he'd worn a sign reading 'No Trespassing' he couldn't have made his untouchability more clear.

'What in the world is going on?' Peggy asked in bewilderment. 'Is there something you haven't told me?'

Jennie turned to her and gave her a puzzled look. 'What do you mean?'

Peggy shrugged and set the plates down on the now empty table. 'Well, the way everyone scattered the minute I showed up, I figured I must have a social problem of some kind.'

Jennie smiled. 'No. Just a slight accident. Nothing serious. Shall we sit down and eat?'

After supper, they wandered out into the crowd thronging the streets, and made their way towards the dance at the far end. Jennie had had more to drink than she was used to, and was glad of the fresh air.

She was also enjoying herself more than she'd thought she would. It was good to see her old friends again, and they all seemed glad to see her. No one mentioned the fiasco of her ruined marriage plans, and for the first time since it had happened she felt that it was finally fading into a dim memory, that she really had recovered from the blow.

As they approached the dance area, the crowd grew thicker, and the music louder, and the minute they reached it Peggy was grabbed and swept away by an old flame of hers. Jennie stood and watched them a little wistfully as they twirled off among the other dancers. Alone for the first time since they had arrived, she wandered around by herself for a few minutes, feeling rather lost, until she came to the canopied bar set up along the sidelines.

'What'll it be, Jennie?' asked the smiling bartender.

It had grown a little chilly, and she pulled the white shawl closer around her shoulders. Also, her head was still a little muddled from the beer, and a cup of coffee or tea sounded good.

'Do you have anything hot to drink, Ken?' she asked.

'Coffee OK?'

She nodded.

'Coming right up, then.'

While she waited for her coffee, she turned round to watch for Peggy, and to her horror found herself staring directly into the eyes of Peter Fleming.

Stifling a little cry, she put a hand to her throat and instinctively stepped back a pace. He looked just the same, with the regular features and sandy hair, the crooked boyish smile, tentative now as he searched her face. Exactly the same, she thought, and all the old pain came flooding back into her heart, filling her whole being with the terrible reminder of her failure.

For a moment she was afraid she might burst into tears or pass out on the spot. He took a step towards her, and it was then that she noticed the tall blonde at his side. His new love, she thought, and that made it even worse.

'Hello, Jennie,' he said, peering anxiously down at her. 'How are you?'

She had to say something, but she was terrified that she wouldn't be able to croak out a word. Trying desperately to hide her confusion, she cleared her throat nervously and forced out a smile.

'I'm fine, Peter. How about you?'

'Oh, I'm OK. You're looking well.' He returned her smile. 'That's quite a costume you've got on.'

Immediately her face went up in flame. She cursed Peggy silently for talking her into wearing the hateful red dress, which by now surely looked like a damp, limp dishcloth. What made it even worse was the costume the blonde had on: a well-tailored pair of flaring black gaucho pants, high-heeled black boots, a flowing, ruffled white silk shirt, and a dashing black Mexican hat tied under her chin.

'Er, Jennie,' Peter said, turning to the blonde, 'I'd like to have you meet Sheila, my, er. . .' He couldn't quite get the word out. 'Sheila, this is Jennie Corbett.'

The blonde Sheila nodded coolly at Jennie, her fine aristocratic nose lifted slightly, a smile of unconcealed triumph hovering about her wide, perfect mouth.

Jennie prayed that the earth would open up and swallow her. She was filled with self-loathing. The terrible dress, her tongue-tied awkwardness, the stark contrast between her own cheap, dishevelled appearance and Peter's svelte, expensive new love. No wonder he'd dumped her. She didn't blame him.

She knew with a kind of defeated resignation that in the next moment she would burst into tears, and was just about to turn and run before she disgraced herself absolutely when she felt a firm arm come around her waist, pulling her towards a hard, masculine chest.

'There you are,' came a vaguely familiar masculine voice. 'I've been looking all over for you.'

Totally taken aback, Jennie jerked her head around to look into the grinning face of Mark Doyle.

CHAPTER THREE

OF ALL the people in Santa Lucia—in the whole *world*—Mark was the last one she would have expected to come to her rescue. She wasn't going to quibble, however, and without a word she sank against him with a sigh of relief.

As he held her tightly around the shoulder, one hand gripping her bare upper arm, he held out his other hand to a goggling Peter. 'Hi,' he said. 'I'm Mark Doyle.'

'Peter Fleming,' the other man murmured.

'Oh, sure,' Mark went on as they shook hands. 'Jennie's spoken of you.' He chuckled. 'Weren't you two childhood sweethearts or something like that?'

'Something like that,' Peter replied in a bewildered tone.

While Peter introduced Mark to Sheila and the three of them chatted, Jennie gradually began to regain her composure. Bless you, Mark! she kept saying over and over again to herself. You really came through when I needed you.

The next thing she knew, Peter had said goodbye and was walking off with the gorgeous Sheila. Jennie hadn't uttered one word during the entire conversation. Still weak with relief, she looked up at Mark.

'Thanks, Mark,' she said with feeling. 'That's one of the nicest things anyone's ever done for me.'

He shrugged and grinned down at her. 'What are friends for?' he asked. 'To tell you the truth, I didn't

43

like the way that wimp was showing off the blonde to you. I'm no angel, but that stinks. Besides,' he went on, the grin broadening, 'I've been watching you in that red dress.' He raised an eyebrow. 'Quite a transformation!'

Jennie noticed then that his arm was still holding her firmly around the shoulder. 'Don't even mention this dress,' she said bitterly. 'It's caused me nothing but grief since I put it on.'

'Well, I'll have to admit that it's a departure from your usual style, but it's very becoming.' The leer he gave her was unmistakable, and Jennie began to wonder if she hadn't jumped out of the frying pan into the fire. 'Come on,' he said. 'I'll buy you a drink and then we can dance.'

'I've already ordered coffee,' she said.

'Fine.' He turned to the bar, where the coffee-cup still sat steaming. He picked it up and held it out to the bartender. 'Lace this with a little bourbon, will you, Ken? And make mine the same.'

Jennie was just about to protest, but then she thought, Why not? She'd played it safe all her life, and look where it had got her. Jilted! Practically left at the altar. And just when Peter had been rubbing her nose in it with his new blonde, along had come Mark to rescue her. So what if he made a pass at her? Maybe it was about time someone did!

By the time they'd finished the heavily laced coffee, Jennie was feeling no more pain at all. They danced for a while, then had another drink, then danced again, and by this time it was almost midnight. She had completely lost track of Peggy, but assumed that she had found her interesting man, and, besides, Peggy was well able to take care of herself.

While they danced, Mark pressed himself closely up against her, and was now moving one large hand up and down her back, over her bare shoulders, then down to her waist again, hesitating just above her hips. She had dropped the lace shawl somewhere along the line, but was so warm by now from the liquor and the heat from Mark's body that she didn't miss it.

Mark had slowly been guiding her over towards the ring of spectators watching the dancing, and when they reached it he stopped abruptly, took her by the hand and pulled her along with him through the crowd. Unthinking, her head still a little fuzzy from drink, and very grateful to him for rescuing her from the awkward scene with Peter, she followed him along towards an isolated shadowy corner under the shade of a sprawling pepper tree.

There was a slight ringing in her ears that muffled the music and the noise of the crowd, and when they reached the tree and Mark pulled her round with him to the other side of the broad, gnarled trunk she didn't even think to wonder why.

As soon as they were safely behind the tree, out of sight of the others, Mark placed his hands on her shoulders and began to knead them gently, his fingers warm on her bare shoulders.

'You look terrific in that red dress,' he said. 'Quite a transformation from the Jennie I'm used to seeing in your father's office.' His hooded eyes glinted appreciatively, flicking her up and down, and he thrust his lower body suggestively against hers.

Jennie's head was reeling. Virtually without any erotic experience at all, she was torn between pleasure at the warm feelings he was evoking in her and a nagging twinge of fear in the pit of her stomach. She was dimly worried that she was getting in over her head with a man who was obviously an expert at seduction, but at the same time flattered by his sudden interest in her.

She gazed up at him uncertainly, her eyes wide, her lips twitching nervously. Then he smiled, and as his head bent down to press his open mouth on hers, the hands on her shoulders slid down to cover her breasts.

Alarmed, she made a choking kind of gasp deep in her throat and tried to pull back from him. He was moving way too fast for her. As she struggled, one arm snaked around her waist, holding her fast, pulling her even closer. When she felt his tongue push past her lips and his other hand slip inside the bodice of her dress, she jerked her head back with all her strength.

'No, Mark!' she cried. 'Stop! Please, stop.'

'Come on, Jennie,' he murmured silkily in her ear. The hand at her waist slid down over her hips. 'What are you afraid of? I won't hurt you.'

She kept struggling in his arms, fruitlessly, powerless against his superior strength. This was far more than she'd bargained for, not what she'd wanted at all. Then she thought, why not? At least Mark wants me when no one else does.

She had just about made up her mind to relax and let him do whatever he wanted when another pair of hands gripped her arms from behind, pulling her away from Mark, and a low, commanding voice rang out.

'OK, Doyle, you heard the lady. That's enough. Leave her alone.'

Half relieved, half angry, Jennie turned her head to see Alex Knight standing behind her, his lean face set in a hard, angry frown, glaring over her head at Mark in a distinctly menacing fashion.

She looked back at Mark, who was slowly retreating, his hands raised defensively in front of him. 'OK, OK,' he said. He gave Alex a weak grin. 'No need to call in the marines. I didn't mean any harm.' His eyes flicked downwards to Jennie. 'Besides, the "lady" seemed willing enough to me.'

Then, with a defiant toss of his head, he turned and stalked off. It had all happened so fast that it wasn't until he disappeared in the crowd surrounding the dancers that Jennie realised Alex was still holding her arms in an iron grip, his fingers digging painfully into her bare flesh.

It was then that anger triumphed. She wriggled free, then turned round to face him, with her hands on her hips and her eyes blazing fire.

'Just what do you think you're doing, Alex?' she sputtered furiously. 'What right——'

'Look at you!' he thundered, his voice throbbing with anger of his own. 'You look like a tramp. Your dress is torn, you're half naked, and you were just about to make a fool of yourself.'

Shocked at the unfamiliar display of emotion from the normally silent, reserved man, Jennie glanced down at her dress. In the scuffle with Mark, one shoulder-strap had broken loose and was hanging down, exposing a good portion of one small, firm breast. Somehow she'd lost one shoe, and there was a rip in her skirt from the hem almost to her thigh.

At the sight, she suddenly sobered. Hot waves of shame washed over her. She pulled the broken strap up, holding it tightly to cover herself, and glared at Alex.

'What business is it of yours?' she demanded in a high, quavering voice. 'I can take care of myself.'

'Sure you can,' he countered caustically. He slipped out of his lightweight jacket, put it around her shoulders, then gripped her by the arm again and turned her around bodily. He started walking away from the dance, pulling her along beside him.

'Where are you taking me?' she cried, dragging her feet. 'You have no right——'

'I'm taking you home where you belong,' he said flatly, and continued on. After a few more steps he broke his stride and gave her a withering glance. 'Where your father is waiting up for you.'

She glared up at him. 'My father has never waited up for me in his life!' she exclaimed. She tried to stamp her foot, but when her bare sole came down on a sharp rock she couldn't stifle the sudden cry of pain.

Alex sighed disgustedly when he saw what had happened, then muttering under his breath about little girls who weren't even capable of keeping their shoes on, reached down, picked her up bodily, and strode purposefully down a back street.

Although Jennie made it as difficult as possible for him, squirming and kicking in his arms, beating ineffectually at his chest and shoulders, she knew when she was beaten, and by the time they reached his station-wagon she was ready to give in. He set her down on the pavement to open the door, still holding on to her.

She shook herself free. 'Let me go,' she said irritably. 'I can get in by myself.'

Without a word, he dropped his hand from her arm, but stood there waiting until she'd climbed inside the car. He shut the door behind her, then strode round to get in on his side, started the engine, then drove off.

They covered the short distance to her house in stony silence, Alex gazing straight ahead, with his eyes fixed on the road and a brooding frown still on his face, Jennie pouting in the corner as far away from him as she could get.

When he parked the car in front of her house and switched off the engine, he sat there for a moment, still deep in thought, his hands on the steering-wheel. Jennie glanced over at him. Under the street-light, she could see that his knuckles were white where he gripped the wheel and a little pulse twitched along his lean jaw.

'You know, you really hurt me back there,' she said sulkily.

He turned on her, his grey eyes blazing. 'Good!' he bit out. 'I should have turned you over my knee and spanked you.'

'Why?' she demanded angrily. 'I was managing quite nicely on my own. I don't need you to——'

'As I recall,' he broke in flatly, 'you were begging him to stop when I came on the scene.'

'It's still none of your business. And what were you doing there in the first place?' She gave him a suspicious look. 'Were you following me?'

A sheepish look appeared fleetingly on his face, and he turned his head away. 'Someone has to,' he muttered. 'You obviously don't know how to take care of yourself, and a cheap one-night stand with a man like Mark Doyle isn't the way to learn.'

'That's my business, isn't it? The minute a man pays a little attention to me, you have to come charging in there and ruin it for me.' It was true, she thought, remembering how grateful she'd felt for Mark's interest in her. 'Mark *likes* me,' she went on heatedly. 'I'm not stupid, you know. I'm well aware that Mark's strongest feeling for me is physical attraction, but can't you understand how grateful I was that *someone* desired me? That even a one-night stand would be a boost to my ego at this point?' Her voice broke as the tears of self-pity began to gather behind her eyes, tears she'd thought she'd conquered for good.

'Jennie,' he said, 'don't. Please, don't cry.'

This display of sympathy only made her feel even more sorry for herself. 'You don't know what it's like to be jilted,' she blubbered.

Alex reached out a hand tentatively towards her, then withdrew it quickly and looked away. 'As it happens,' he said in a hard, flat voice, 'I do.'

That got her attention. She stopped crying immediately and stared wonderingly at him. 'What do you mean by that?'

'Nothing. You'd better go in now. Your father will be worried about you.'

'I told you. He never worries about me. I want to know what you meant by that statement.'

'It's nothing,' he said harshly. 'I'm just getting a little sick of your self-pity. You need to understand that you're not the only person in the world who's ever suffered. You're young. You'll get over it. Some things never go away,' he added bitterly. 'You just have to learn to live with them forever.'

The bitterness in his voice astounded her. She'd always felt that there was some mystery about Alex. No one seemed to know where he came from or what his past life had been before he'd arrived in Santa Lucia seven or eight years ago—not even her father, who was probably his closest friend.

It was then that she remembered the scar she'd seen earlier when Betty Furlong had torn his shirt. He'd obviously gone home to change it, and she realised with a slight shock that he'd also shaved off his beard while he was at it. Completely sober by now, she also began to feel a little ashamed of her childish behaviour. Still, she wasn't ready to give in quite yet.

'That's very comforting,' she said sarcastically. 'And easy for you to say. Just how am I supposed to get over the fact that Peter doesn't want me any more? Please explain to me how I'm going to live with the knowledge that no man ever will want me.'

'Damn it, Jennie!' he ground out, turning on her angrily. 'You're just being childish again. What makes you think no man will ever want you? That's the most stupid thing I've ever heard. If nothing else, Mark Doyle's behaviour tonight should have proved to you that you're a desirable young woman.'

'Oh, sure,' she sneered. 'A minute ago you were warning me off men like Mark and their one-night stands.'

He stared fixedly at her for a long moment. Then gave her a menacing half-smile. 'You want a one-night stand, Jennie? OK, I'm a man. I'll give it to you.'

Before she could grasp what he meant he had reached out for her, pulled her roughly towards him and covered her mouth with his in a hard, grinding, punishing kiss. Shocked beyond words, she simply went limp, and as the kiss went on and on, his lips moving against hers, his teeth biting into the inside of her mouth, an odd feeling began to creep over her.

This was nothing like Peter's tepid, almost brotherly kisses, nor Mark's impulsive, practised, seductive technique. This was a *man* kissing her. The roughness of his recently shaved face rasped against her cheek, the fresh clean scent of his skin and hair filled her nostrils, and she was filled with wonder at how *right* it seemed to be in the arms of a man whom she'd never thought of as a lover.

Finally, he jerked his head back and pushed her away at the same time. Their eyes met. She could hear his laboured breathing, feel the quickened pace of her own heartbeat. Slowly, she raised her hand and brushed her fingers across her bruised lips.

'Is that what you want, Jennie?' he asked harshly. Then, suddenly, he threw back his head and laughed. 'Fun and games are over for tonight,' he said derisively at last. 'I only hope you've learned your lesson. Now it's time to go in, little girl.'

If he had slapped her, she couldn't have felt more stunned. 'You beast!' she said. 'I'll never speak to you again, Alex Knight.'

She opened the car door, got out, and started running up the path to the house, limping as she went because of the lost shoe. His laughter followed her all the way inside, until she slammed the door behind her and leaned up against it, panting with fury.

Much as she hated to admit it, by the next morning, after waking from a deep, exhausted sleep, Jennie realised that not only had Alex been right to pry her away from Mark Doyle, but that she had indeed learned a lesson from what had happened between them later in his car. A bitter lesson, to be sure, and one she would never forgive him for entirely, but for some reason she woke up feeling better about herself and her life than she had for weeks.

The next day was Sunday, and when she went downstairs to the kitchen, only slightly hung over, her father was already there, deep in the enormous San

Francisco newspaper and tucking into a large plate of bacon and eggs.

'Well, how was the dance?' he asked.

'Oh, you know how those things are,' she said with an offhand gesture. 'Pretty rowdy.' As she passed by him on the way to the refrigerator to pour herself some much needed orange juice, she took a closer look at him. 'Dad, are you feeling all right?'

'Sure,' he replied quickly. 'Why do you ask?'

She frowned at him. 'I don't know. You left early last night, and you've seemed tired lately. Are you sure you should be working so hard?'

'Hah!' he snorted. 'I have a pretty easy time of it.'

Just then the telephone rang. No one but Peggy ever called that early, and it suddenly dawned on Jennie that she'd lost track of her friend early in the evening. If she knew Peggy, she'd better get some explanations all ready before she answered.

'I'll get that, Dad,' she said, running out into the hall where she would have some privacy.

It was indeed Peggy, and she was full of accusations. 'Well, what in the world happened to you last night?' she demanded indignantly. 'I looked all over for you after the dance, and finally left by myself. I take it you got home all right.'

'I'm sorry, Peggy. I got side-tracked.'

'What do you mean? Do I sense a man in the picture?'

'Well. . .' Jennie hedged.

'Come on, give. What happened?'

'Why don't you come over later this morning and I'll tell you all about it? Right now I desperately need some sustenance.' She paused for a moment. 'I think I must be a little hung over. My head aches and the inside of my mouth feels like something dead has been decaying in it for a month.'

Peggy chuckled gleefully. 'Had a little too much to drink last night, I take it. Shame on you.'

'Something like that. Anyway, give me a few hours to get dressed and brush my teeth and try to get some food down.'

'Drink tons of coffee and juice.'

Jennie groaned. 'It was the coffee I had last night that did me in.' She forced out a weak smile. 'Although I think there must have been as much bourbon in it as there was coffee.'

'Well, try it this time without the bourbon.'

Two hours later, they were out in the back garden under the shade of the jacaranda tree sipping lemonade. It was going to be another blistering hot day, the noon sun high in the sky and already beating down mercilessly. The still air was heavy with the scent of roses, and, except for the whirr of the grasshoppers in the uncut lawn, it was very quiet, with only an occasional car passing by on the street in front of the house.

'So what happened after I left to dance?' Peggy asked. She was lying on the grass, propped up on one elbow and gazing at Jennie, who was stretched out on a chaise-longue.

'Well, if you can believe it, the first thing I did was run smack into Peter and his new love.'

Peggy pushed herself bolt upright and stared. 'You're kidding,' she breathed. Her expression hardened. 'He's got some nerve, showing his face around here after the dirty trick he pulled on you. It's a wonder the town doesn't tar and feather him.'

'Oh, come on, Peggy. His family still lives here, after

all. He has a perfect right to be here. Leaving a girl at the altar isn't exactly a capital crime,' she added lightly.

'Well, what was she like?' Peggy asked curiously.

'About what you'd expect. Blonde, gorgeous, expensive. Her name is Sheila.'

Peggy snorted. 'And I suppose it's only coincidence that her father happens to be chief of staff of the hospital in San Francisco that offered Peter that plummy residency.'

Jennie smiled. 'Now, how do you know that?'

'Honey, this is Santa Lucia, remember? Everyone here knows everything about everyone else.' She gave Jennie a searching look. 'How did it feel to run into them like that? Was it awful for you?'

'At first it was. I was so surprised to see them that it really threw me off balance there for a while.' She sighed and gazed up at the blue canopy of jacaranda blossoms overhead. 'I guess I'll always love Peter in a way, and it did hurt to see him with another woman. We'd been together for so long, it just didn't seem natural——'

She broke off then as the old ache began to clutch at her heart once again. Then she realised that at least she was able to talk about it, that the expected tears didn't fall, that the hurt was actually healing.

'So then what happened?' Peggy asked softly.

Jennie laughed. 'Well, just as it was getting really sticky, along came Mark Doyle, of all people, to the rescue.'

'Mark Doyle?' Peggy exclaimed. 'The octopus himself—all hands. You'd better watch out for him.'

Jennie flushed at the reminder of what had happened later, and hastened on. 'Anyway, Mark made a big fuss over me, as though he'd been looking for me all night.

I wish you could have seen the look on Peter's face. It was so funny.'

'It was the red dress!' Peggy said smugly. 'I told you it did wonders for you.' She searched Jennie's face. 'So did you and Mark, um, you know?'

'No! Of course not!' She had no intention of telling Peggy just how close she'd come to 'you know' just a short time later.

'Then how *did* you get home? Walk?'

Jennie raised her glass and took a long swallow of lemonade to hide her embarrassment, then murmured, 'Oh, I ran into Alex Knight, Dad's friend, and he gave me a ride home.'

'Now there's an interesting man,' Peggy stated. 'Deep. Mysterious. I think there's a thrilling secret in his past.'

'What makes you say that?' Jennie asked quickly.

'Oh, you know,' Peggy replied with an offhand shrug. 'He's lived in Santa Lucia for—how long? Seven, eight years? And no one to my knowledge has ever seen him with a woman. He just stays out at that winery of his like some kind of recluse.' She rolled over on her stomach and gazed up at Jennie. 'What's he like? I mean, what did you talk about?'

'Nothing much,' Jennie said airily. Her cheeks were burning again at the memory of that heated argument in Alex's car, the punishing kiss, the sound of his laughter following her into the house. 'He's just a friend of Dad's.'

Peggy jumped up and brushed the loose grass off her bare legs. 'I'm broiling out here. Let's go down to the lake and have a swim.'

Relieved to have the subject dropped, Jennie got up from the chaise-longue. 'Good idea,' she said.

* * *

The next day was business as usual in her father's office, and Jennie was glad to get back to work. It still wasn't entirely clear to her just what had happened at the dance on Saturday night. She hadn't seen Alex since, and was curious as to how they would react to each other when they did meet.

She'd been busy all morning, ushering her father's patients into the examination rooms, filling in her charts, soothing a sobbing child after a smallpox vaccination, and by noon the last appointment of the morning had left. She straightened her desk and was about to go and ask her father if he wanted to have lunch at home that day when the bell at the top of the door jangled.

She turned around to see Mark Doyle shuffle slowly inside. For a moment they only stared at each other. Then laughter began to bubble up inside her at the sheepish, hangdog expression on his face. Squelching it down, she gave him a solemn look.

'Good morning, Mark,' she said.

'Hi, Jennie,' he said in a low voice. He slowly walked over to the desk and stared down at it, fiddling with the stapler. Then he raised his eyes and said, 'I guess I owe you an apology for the other night. I think I got out of line.'

'No apology needed, Mark,' she said cheerfully. 'It was the *fiesta*. We all do things we wouldn't do ordinarily.' She laughed. 'I know I did. That laced coffee was powerful stuff.'

Relief washed over his face, and he gave her a grateful smile. 'Well, that's all right, then. I had a little too much to drink myself.' He eyed her thoughtfully. 'Besides, that dress you had on was pretty tempting.

And I'm not known for my ability to resist any kind of temptation.'

The clear implication was that today, dressed as usual in a neat blue skirt and striped cotton blouse, she had no power to inspire passion in even the most lustful of men, and the realisation was vaguely depressing to her.

'Well, I'm glad to see you have yourself well under control,' she remarked drily.

He gave her a bewildered look, then raised his hand to rub it along the back of his neck. 'Hell, Jennie, I didn't mean——' He broke off. 'What I meant to say was that I ordinarily don't think of you as that kind of girl. That under normal circumstances I never would have tried anything with you. You know what I mean.' He shrugged helplessly.

'Yes, Mark,' she said with a inward sigh of resignation, 'I know what you mean.'

He brightened. 'Then we're still friends?'

'Right, Mark. Still friends.'

'Good. Now, is your dad in? I have a new line of antibiotics just approved by the Food and Drug Administration that I think he'd be interested in.'

'Yes, he's in his office.'

With another grateful smile and an insouciant wave of his hand, Mark walked past her towards her father's office.

When he had gone, Jennie stood at the desk, unmoving. She didn't know what she had expected, but the conversation with Mark had left her filled with depressing thoughts. She told herself that she wasn't interested in Mark Doyle anyway, not with his reputation, and there certainly was no hope of any kind of future with him. Still, it would have been nice to be at least pursued, even by 'the octopus', and it rankled that he didn't even consider her worth seducing!

For the next few days, Jennie found herself merely going through the motions of her daily life, the vague sense of oppression never quite leaving her. She felt as if she were existing in a kind of vacuum, filled with vague longings which she couldn't quite define. Nothing really interested her. The past was dead, and all her hopes along with it, and the future yawned ahead of her, bleak and empty.

Although she didn't know what it was that she wanted, it was painfully clear that she wasn't likely to get it, whatever it was. She no longer yearned for Peter. That was over for good, and after actually seeing him with Sheila she could accept it at last.

On Thursday night after dinner, feeling restless, she asked her father if he would like to go to the cinema with her. He gave her a shocked look across the table.

'It's Thursday, Jennie. Tonight is our chess night.'

'I'm sorry, Dad. I forgot.'

She got up to clear away the dinner dishes, wondering how in the world it could have slipped her mind that Alex would be coming tonight for his weekly chess game. As she rinsed off the dishes at the sink, she thought about the last time she had seen him. It would be too humiliating to see him again after what had happened that night. She would just have to avoid him.

Just then the doorbell rang.

'Would you get that, honey?' her father called. 'I want to go up and get this suit and tie off.'

She turned around to protest, but he was already half-way up the stairs on his way to his bedroom. She had no choice. Wiping her hands dry, she walked slowly down the hall to the front door. She stood there for a moment, then took a deep breath and opened it.

He looked just the same as always, she thought, gazing up at him. Tall and lean and tanned, dressed as usual in dark trousers and a long-sleeved white shirt, the top button undone at the throat, the sleeves rolled up to his elbows, and the familiar shut-in, distant expression firmly fixed on his face.

Yet there was a difference. Not only was she intensely aware now of the long scar underneath the carefully buttoned shirt, but also of that wide thin mouth that had once pressed against hers, the smooth-shaven jaw that had scraped her skin, the watchful grey eyes that had glinted at her in anger. She realised then that she was actually seeing him with new eyes, seeing him as a live flesh-and-blood man, and not just as her father's friend.

'Hello, Jennie,' he said easily.

'Alex,' she murmured as he stepped inside.

'Your father is expecting me,' he said when she'd closed the door behind him.

She turned to him and said stiffly, 'Yes, I know.'

There was a short, awkward silence as she waited for him to go on, but it soon became clear that he wasn't going to say anything more, certainly nothing personal.

She walked past him and started for the kitchen. 'I was just straightening up after dinner,' she called over her shoulder as she went. 'Would you like a cup of coffee?'

'Yes, thank you. I would,' he replied.

He followed her into the kitchen and stood at the window, looking out at the garden, his hands in the back pockets of his trousers, while she poured his coffee.

'Sit down,' she said. 'I'm almost through in here, and Dad will be down soon. He just went up to change his clothes.'

He turned to take the cup from her, but made no move to sit down. He raised the cup to his lips, took a sip, then said, 'I wanted to have a word with you, Jennie. Do you have a minute?'

'Yes. Yes, of course,' she replied nervously.

She looked at him, searching his face for some sign of what he had on his mind, but could read nothing in the remote expression, the stony grey eyes. Suddenly her knees felt weak, her heart started to pound erratically, and she gripped the back of a chair to steady herself.

Here it comes, she thought, totally in the dark as to what 'it' might be, but full of trepidation about it. Somehow she had the vague idea that he was going to scold her again for throwing herself at Mark Doyle or, worse, launch into an explanation of the part he himself had played later in that little drama, and, full of fear and trembling, she primed herself to do battle.

CHAPTER FOUR

'It's about your father,' he said, settling himself at the table.

'My father?' She stood looking down at him in bewilderment.

'Yes. I don't mean to alarm you, but I'm sure you realise that his health is not good. Is there any way you can get him to take it easier?'

She sank slowly down on the chair beside him. After that one mild heart attack she had been worried about her father, but lately she had been so full of her own problems that she'd almost forgotten about it. The plan was to have been that Peter would join him in the autumn and relieve him of much of the burden of his practice. But that was a thing of the past now, and the last subject in the world she wanted to discuss with Alex Knight.

'I don't know,' she said slowly. 'I can try, but he's awfully stubborn.' She gave him a worried look. 'Do you think it's serious? I mean, is there immediate danger?'

'I don't know. I'm not a doctor. He is. If anyone knows just how sick he is, he should.'

'I'll talk to him,' Jennie said. 'See if I can get him to cut down on his practice. I know he'll never give it up entirely.'

Just then she heard her father's footsteps coming slowly down the stairs. She looked at Alex, who was staring at her with an odd, quizzical expression on his lean face.

'There's one more thing,' he said in a low voice.

Jennie steeled herself. He was going to bring up the fiasco at the dance after all, and she didn't want to talk about that with him, either. Well, there was no law that said she had to. If he started playing the heavy-handed father-figure again, scolding her for her behaviour, she would just tell him to mind his own business.

'What is it?' she asked stiffly.

I wanted to apologise for the way I yanked you away from Mark Doyle the other night and manhandled you that way.' He smiled bleakly. 'I don't ordinarily act on impulse like that, but you're so young, Jennie, so untouched by life, that I was afraid you were getting in over your head. At any rate, I had no right to interfere.' He shrugged. 'Chalk it up to my friendship with your father, or frustrated paternal instinct. If I spoiled a budding romance for you, I'm sorry.'

Jennie could hardly believe her ears. This polite apology was the last thing she had expected from him. She stared blankly at him, unable to utter a word, watching him as he rose to his feet, drained his coffee and set the cup down on the counter-top.

Then, from the hallway just outside the kitchen, came her father's voice. 'Alex?' he called. 'Are you ready to start?'

'Coming,' Alex called. He looked at Jennie. 'Are we friends again, Jennie?' he asked softly.

Friends? she thought. When had they ever been friends? She gave him a tight smile. 'Yes. Yes, of course.'

'Good.' With that, he strode past her towards the hall, speaking to her father as he went.

When he had gone Jennie continued to sit at the table, staring into space and listening to the low voices of the two men as they chatted on their way to the study.

The brief conversation had left her more confused than ever about this strange, secretive man, and as she pondered it in her mind, going back over the heated scene in his car on the night of the dance, it dawned on her that he hadn't uttered one word about *his* sudden flare-up, that one punishing kiss, or about the allusions he had made to his own mysterious past.

Men! she thought disgustedly. She got up, went out into the hall and started climbing the stairs to her room. She was better off without the whole dreary, frustrating lot of them! Peter, with his sudden abandonment of all their lovely plans; Mark Doyle, with his egotistical, single-minded lechery; and Alex Knight, with his scar, the past he wouldn't talk about, and his bland assumption that nothing had passed between them the other night.

Well, maybe nothing had. She'd had too much to drink, and had still been reeling from seeing Peter with his Sheila and the struggle with Mark. Maybe she'd dreamed the whole thing. *He* certainly acted as though it had never happened.

What was more to the point, and clearly the most urgent matter, was his warning about her father's health. She would have to have a talk with him about taking it easier. For all the good it would do her! He was the most stubborn of the whole bunch of them.

'Men!' she muttered again under her breath, and went into the bathroom to run a hot bath.

* * *

After that night, Jennie's life settled down into a dull routine where, even though she wasn't really happy, neither was she suffering any more from that first excruciating pain of rejection.

At the first opportunity she did speak to her father about slowing down, taking it easier, perhaps even retiring. As she fully expected, he only gazed at her in horror and flatly refused even to consider any of her ideas.

'I might as well shoot myself right now and be done with it!' he exclaimed in no uncertain terms.

She never raised the subject again, but she did keep a more careful eye on him, watching his diet, taking on as much of the burden of his practice as she was capable of handling herself, seeing that he got plenty of rest.

As the days and weeks passed, she slowly began to get used to the idea that she was most likely doomed to a life without love, and was actually grateful that she at least had her father to look after.

A few times, under Peggy's prompting, she toyed with the idea of continuing her education at the nearby junior college, but couldn't seem to work up the energy or enthusiasm necessary for such a drastic step.

She cooked and cleaned for her father, worked long hours in his office, gardened a little, read a lot. She and Peggy would go out to the cinema once in a while, or attend a picnic with their old gang from school, and she tried to convince herself that she was contented with her life.

And so, summer passed into autumn. She never heard from or about Peter, and assumed that by now he and his new love were happily married. Although Mark Doyle would breeze back in town about once a month on one of his regular selling jaunts, he treated her as he always had, in a joking, teasing, brotherly fashion, as though the night of the dance had never happened.

Alex, of course, had slipped effortlessly back into his old role of family friend, something like her father's younger brother, a rather distant uncle. He appeared regularly for the weekly chess sessions or an occasional dinner, treating Jennie, as always, with the familiar courteous restraint.

It seemed wonderful to her what convenient memories men had. In her increasingly rare bouts of lingering self-pity and bitterness, she had to struggle against a sudden powerful urge to murder the whole lot of them, and even, in her fantasies, considered the best method of doing so, usually deciding on poison as the most effective and least traceable.

These ferocious impulses served as a kind of catharsis for her, so ridiculous that she could laugh at herself for even thinking them, and eventually even that little bit of excitement was dropped from her life.

One night in early October, she was walking home from work in an early twilight, wondering what to prepare for dinner, and whether she should stop at the grocer's for something different, when the sudden shrill wail of a siren pierced the stillness.

She was almost at her street by now, a quiet neighbourhood of elderly frame-houses with neat front gardens and spreading trees at the kerb. There was a nip in the air, and, shivering a little in her thin sweater and light cotton dress, she quickened her step as the siren grew louder.

As she hurried forward, somehow she knew, even before she turned the corner and caught sight of the flashing blue lights on the ambulance parked in front of the house, and she instinctively slowed her pace, as though to delay the moment when she would have to face the dreadful truth.

A small cluster of neighbours were gathered on the pavement in front of the house, craning their necks and whispering among themselves. Unseeing, Jennie walked slowly past them, dimly aware of their sympathetic stares, her mind already preparing itself for the inevitable.

She met the medics at the door. They were carrying a stretcher, a still form clearly outlined beneath the white sheet. After the first glance, Jennie turned stricken eyes on the white-coated man in front.

'Sorry, Jennie,' he said. 'We did everything we could.'

Everyone was very helpful. Dr Corbett had been a well-loved fixture in Santa Lucia for so long that friends appeared out of nowhere, all eager to do what they could, and, although Jennie was always tactfully asked what her wishes were in each decision that had to be made, all the practical details of death's aftermath were taken care of for her.

He died on a Wednesday; the funeral was held on Friday. During the intervening day, Jennie moved like a zombie, going through the motions of daily life mechanically, still unable to take in the fact that her father was really gone.

After the funeral, there was a short reception back at the house, prepared by Peggy and a few of the neighbours. They were all very kind, treating Jennie with sympathetic deference, speaking in low, hushed tones as they stood in the reception line to offer her their condolences, then later milled around drinking coffee and picking at the sandwiches and cakes spread out on the dining-table.

Alex was there, of course, gaunt and haggard with his own grief at the loss of his friend, and more withdrawn than ever. Jennie had caught a glimpse of him at the funeral as principal pallbearer, tall and monkish-looking in his dark suit and tie, but, after murmuring a few brief words of sympathy to her at the reception, he vanished.

Jennie, still stunned, had to make a heroic effort to show her gratitude to the crowd that had gathered to pay its last respects to the beloved doctor, but as she stood in the living-room greeting each guest all she could think of was how relieved she would be when they all left and she could be alone with her sorrow.

Mechanically, she thanked each guest in line, shaking their hands, trying to smile, longing for it to be over, and it was with a slight sense of shock that she found herself looking straight into the light blue eyes of Peter Fleming.

He reached out to grasp her hand in both of his and leaned down to kiss her lightly on the cheek. 'Jen,' he said in a low voice, 'I'm so sorry.'

Jennie gazed stonily at him. Somehow in her dazed grief she blamed him for everything. If he had remained true to his commitments, kept his promises, they would be married by now, he would be helping with the practice, and her father would still be alive.

'Hello, Peter,' she said coldly. Then, at the look of misery and guilt on his face, she realised how pointless it was to blame him, or anyone else, and added, 'Thank you for coming.'

He opened his mouth, as though he had more to say,

but the line behind him pressed forward and, with a last gentle squeeze of her hand, he stepped aside.

The real surprise of the long dreary afternoon was the appearance of Mark Doyle, who was the last in line. As they shook hands, Jennie gazed in amazement at the transformation in him. The wild flaming hair was slicked down neatly, he was wearing a conservative grey suit instead of the usual stylish checks and bright colours, and there was a look of subdued solemnity on his normally lively features.

'Please accept my condolences, Jennie,' he said in a stiff, formal voice. 'I—I was very fond of your father.'

'It was nice of you to come, Mark. I appreciate it.'

He nodded grimly and was about to leave, when he reached out to take her hand again, leaned closer and said, 'If there's anything I can do for you, anything you need, you only have to ask.'

Jennie widened her eyes at him. She'd never seen Mark so serious, and she was touched by his obvious emotion.

'Why, thank you, Mark,' she said. 'Thank you very much.'

With another brief nod, he turned and walked away.

At last it was over, the last guest greeted, and she could simply disappear. People had already started to leave. Peggy and the neighbours would clean up after them. Her own role in the whole dreadful drama was over. She wouldn't be missed now if she went up to her own room.

It wasn't until after all the well-wishers had gone and she was alone at last in the big house, its emptiness echoing around her, that the realisation really hit her for the first time. She was all alone in the world now.

There was an aunt, her mother's sister, living in Arizona, a cousin in Los Angeles, but they'd never been close.

Later that night she stood in her father's silent study, surrounded by his books, his desk still littered with his papers. Now all she had to do, she thought as she gazed around at all the familiar objects, was figure out what she was going to do with the rest of her life.

During the next few weeks, Jennie was too busy to worry about her future. Dr Watkins, who had shared her father's office, helped her sort out his belongings. He also offered to keep her on at her old job, but once all the personal things had been cleared away she knew that she couldn't face going back there.

Peggy was her mainstay during those first awful weeks. She made a point of dropping by the house every night on her way home from work, tried to cheer her up, insisted that she eat, and even tried to discuss her future plans, but in late October she, too, had to leave on a buying trip for the dress shop where she worked, and then Jennie really was alone.

As the days passed, she found herself sinking lower and lower into a depression that she couldn't fight. She was sleeping badly and could barely force down the occasional scanty meal she managed to prepare. Even in her exhausted state, she was dimly aware that although she grieved for her father, her *malaise* went much deeper than that.

Quite simply, there didn't seem to be anywhere for her to turn. Nothing interested her. Soon she even stopped getting dressed in the morning, and would lie around the house all day watching silly programmes on the television, leafing through old magazines—any-thing to distract herself from thinking about the future.

Then, on a clear cold night in early November, about a month after the funeral, Alex came to the house. It was early evening, just at the same time as he used to show up for the chess games.

Jennie was very surprised to see him. Although he'd been a great help to her in the immediate aftermath of her father's death, after the funeral he had simply disappeared. She hadn't seen him or heard a word from him since then, and, in fact, in her recent stupor, had quite forgotten that he even existed.

When she opened the door to see him standing there, the collar of his heavy jacket turned up against the hint of frost in the air, his hands stuffed in the pockets, instinctively she half turned to call her father. Then she remembered. Her father was gone, and the awful ache returned to clutch at her heart.

'Hello, Alex,' she said dully.

'Can I come in for a minute, Jennie?'

Wordlessly, she nodded, and he stepped inside, closing the door behind him. She turned and led the way into her father's study, the warmest room in the house and where she had spent most of her time during the past month. She clutched her old blue woollen bathrobe around herself, switched on a light and turned to him.

'Sit down,' she said.

They sat together on the long, shabby couch in front of the dead fireplace. Jennie folded her hands in her lap and waited, wondering what in the world he wanted.

She glanced over at him. He was leaning forward, his elbows on his knees, his hands clasped in front of him, staring broodingly down at the floor. As she examined his pale, drawn features, it suddenly dawned on her that he had grief of his own to contend with, and she softened towards him.

'How have you been, Alex?' she asked at last.

He darted a quick sideways glance at her. 'All right. How about you?'

She shrugged and smiled wanly. 'I'm OK. Everyone tells me that these things take time. I guess I'm waiting for it to pass.'

He nodded and turned to stare down at the floor a few moments more. Then he rose abruptly to his feet and started pacing around the room, stopping occasionally to examine her father's old possessions; the green glass ashtray on the desk, a dead cigar still lying there, the diplomas hanging on the wall, the old wedding photograph on the mantel above the fireplace.

Finally he came to stand before her, his arms hanging loosely at his sides. 'I've been wondering, Jennie, what your plans are.'

She gave him a puzzled look. 'Plans?'

'Yes. For example, are you going to keep the house, stay on here alone?'

'Of course. It's my home.'

'Will you be able to afford it?'

'It's all paid for.'

'Yes, but you'll have to support it—taxes, insurance, upkeep, utilities. And yourself as well—food, clothing. You'll need an income, a job.'

'Yes, I guess so. I hadn't really thought about it. Dr Watkins offered to keep me on, but I don't think I want to do that. Besides, Dad left me enough to get by on for a while. I know it won't last forever, but later on I can probably get a job at the hospital or——' she shrugged helplessly '—somewhere.'

'Is that what you want?'

As she gazed up at him, her eyes suddenly filled with tears. 'I don't know what I want. He's only been gone a month.'

He sat down beside her. 'I know that, Jennie. And I don't mean to rush you. I realise how difficult the last several months have been for you. First calling off your marriage to Peter Fleming, then losing your father. But look at you! You're losing weight, you don't take care of yourself. Jennie, you've got to snap out of it and start living again.'

She glanced down at the shabby bathrobe and ran a hand through her short dark hair, which she hadn't bothered to wash for several days. She probably should be offended, she thought, but couldn't even seem to work up the energy for that. She just gazed up at him wordlessly.

'I only want to help you,' he said in a gentler tone.

'I know that, Alex. And I appreciate it.'

He got up again and walked over to the fireplace. He stood there with his back to her for some time, as though deep in thought, then turned round to face her, his hands clasped behind his back.

'I need some help at the winery,' he said brusquely. 'The business is expanding, and I can't keep track of the books properly. I thought, since you've been used to handling accounts for your father, you might want to tackle the job.'

She stared at him. 'You mean, work for you?'

He nodded. 'For a while, anyway, just to tide you over until you decide what you want to do.' He paused, frowning, then went on, 'I also think you should get out of this house, perhaps find a small apartment, or, if you do decide to come to work for me, I have plenty of room out there. It's not good for a young girl like you to rattle around here all by yourself. Your father always hoped you'd continue your education. Selling the house would give you the wherewithal to do so.'

She was deeply disturbed by his words, and a sense of injury slowly began to build inside her. She wasn't *ready* to make decisions like that! And what business was it of Alex Knight's what she did with her life? Where had he been all these weeks when she'd really needed his support and advice? Seized by a sudden overpowering rush of indignation, she flushed heatedly, and as the anger boiled over she rose to her feet and faced him, her eyes blazing, her hands clenched into fists at her sides.

'That was Dad's idea, my going back to school, not mine. I don't want more education, I don't want a career. You know darned good and well that all I ever had on my mind was marrying Peter, settling down, making a home, having children. If I can't have that, I don't want anything. Now, why don't you just leave me alone?'

He came slowly towards her, and when he reached her she was shocked to see that his lips were twitching, as though he was trying to suppress a smile.

'Well, you'll have to admit,' he said, 'that, offensive as you find my words, they at least got a rise out of you.'

'I don't think it's in the least funny,' she said icily.

'All right,' he said. 'I apologise. Maybe it's too soon.' He sighed, then raised a hand and rubbed it wearily over the back of his neck. 'I know you don't have anyone to advise you, and, as your father's friend, I felt I owed it to him to take on the job. I'm sorry if I presumed too much.'

She couldn't look at him. She just wanted him to leave, and take his advice with him. There was dead silence in the room for a few seconds, then she heard him turn and walk away, heard the front door open and close as he let himself out, and, alone at last, she sank down on the couch and breathed a sigh of relief.

It didn't take long, however, for the utter stillness of the house to close in on her. Somehow, the silence which had been so comforting and reassuring to her before Alex had come, now seemed terribly lonely, even threatening.

She thought over what he had said. Could he be right? It didn't take her long to admit that he probably was. She knew it now, and she had known it even then. It was why she'd reacted with fear and anger to his suggestions. She hadn't wanted to face the necessity of making *any* decisions. Maybe it was about time she learned.

The next morning she got up early, went straight to the bathroom to shower and wash her hair, then got dressed in a clean blue woollen skirt and white tailored blouse. After her hair had dried, she combed it as neatly as possible in its present condition, promising herself to get it cut soon, and went downstairs to prepare herself a real meal.

Then, right after breakfast, she reached for the telephone and dialled Alex's number. She still wasn't sure that she was doing the right thing, but at least she was doing something. During the sleepless night, as she'd mulled over her dwindling options, the one thing that had become clearer and clearer to her was that she couldn't go on in her present situation.

As soon as he answered the telephone, and she heard his deep steady voice come on the line, she plunged right in.

'Alex, this is Jennie. I've been thinking over what you said last night, and wanted to apologise for behaving so badly. I know you were only trying to help.'

'No apology necessary,' came the gruff reply.

'I also wanted to tell you that you were right—I do need to make some decisions, about the house, about my future.' She laughed nervously. 'I guess that when my famous wedding plans fell through I just gave up and started going through the motions. Now, with Dad gone, I realise that I can't do that any more.'

'So,' he said, 'does that mean you'll take the job with me?'

'You really were serious?'

'Of course.'

'And it's not just charity? I mean, you really do need someone? If not, I can probably find some kind of work here in town.'

'No,' he said, 'it's not charity. If it were, I'd just offer you money. I really do need some good office help. My books are in a mess.'

'Well, then, I accept.'

'Good. When can you start?'

She laughed. Suddenly the dismal cloud that had been hovering directly over her head for the past several months seemed to vanish into thin air. 'Right away, I guess.'

'Why don't you drive out here some time today, then, and I'll show you around, give you an idea of what I need? Come for lunch.' He paused for a moment. 'Have you decided what you're going to do about the house?'

'Yes. You were right there, too. I'm going to call the estate agent today and put it on the market.'

'Good. Then I'll help you move your things out here this weekend.'

She'd forgotten all about his suggestion that she stay at his ranch, and she hesitated. She hadn't really thought at all beyond the decision to sell the house, to take the job he had offered her. But to live with him?

As though sensing her hesitation, he went on quickly, 'That's entirely up to you, of course, Jennie. It would be more convenient for you than having to drive all the way out here every day, and only a temporary measure, until you feel able to make other plans.'

For some reason, a sudden picture rose up in her mind of the night of the *fiesta*, way back in July, of Alex snatching her away from Mark Doyle, driving her home, and of the heated argument in his car, the punishing kiss.

Then she heard his low chuckle. 'And you don't have to worry about gossip. My housekeeper, Mrs Anthony, is a pillar of the local church, and as eagle-eyed a chaperon as anyone could wish for.'

Tongue-tied, her mind wandering now to the long scar she'd seen when his shirt was torn and, later, his enigmatic allusion to his own past hurts, she still couldn't say a word.

'Jennie?' he said. 'Are you still there?'

'Yes. I'm sorry. I was wool-gathering.'

'We can talk about living arrangements later. What time can you get out here?'

She glanced at her watch. It was only nine o'clock,

but she had a lot to do. She would have to call the
estate agent, then later on pitch in and give the house
a thorough cleaning before putting it on the market. It
was also time to start clearing out her father's belongings, a task she had been avoiding for weeks, and one
she still dreaded.

'I should be able to make it for lunch,' she said at
last.

'Good. See you then.'

CHAPTER FIVE

AT A quarter to twelve, Jennie set out for Alex's ranch, which lay about ten miles north of town, set in a valley of lush farmland between rolling hills that rose up gently on either side. As she drove along past mile after mile of the vineyards owned by the various wineries in the valley, the grape-vines gnarled and bare now in the harsh November cold, she felt buoyed up with a new sense of purpose and direction.

Although the tasks ahead of her were overwhelming whenever she lumped them all together in her mind, one by one they didn't seem nearly as bad, and after talking to Alex that morning she'd pitched in with a new sense of exhilaration, animated by the mere fact that she was doing *something* positive instead of just sitting around moping.

After she'd spoken to the estate agent, who assured her that she would have no trouble getting a good price for the house, she called Peggy and arranged with her to come over that evening and help her go through her father's things. She just didn't think she could face that sad task by herself.

It had been years since she'd been out to Alex's place. Since he lived as a virtual recluse and did no entertaining whatsoever, there was never any reason to go. In fact, the last time had been five years ago, when she was only eighteen, and she'd ridden out with her father to keep him company.

She slowed down to search the side of the road for

landmarks. Although the terrain was familiar to her, she wasn't sure just which side road led to his place. Then, at a crossroads, she saw an open wooden gate. On one of the posts was a sign, 'Knight Winery', and she made a quick sharp right.

On either side of the narrow, bumpy road stretched mile after mile of vineyard, a familiar sight in the valley. Just ahead was a tall poplar windbreak, with spreading live oak and pepper trees underneath.

Past the trees, at a bend in the road, she finally caught sight of the house, a low, sprawling structure built of rough redwood siding, with a split-cedar shake roof. Smoke was rising up into the cold blue November sky from one of the brick chimneys, and, with no landscaping to speak of, the house had a stark, businesslike air about it.

As she pulled her car into the wide parking area, Alex came out of the house and started walking towards her, one hand raised in greeting. He was dressed in black trousers and a leather jacket lined with sheepskin, his shoulders hunched forwards against the cold.

'Glad you decided to come,' he said, opening the car door.

She stepped out on to the driveway and looked up at him. His face was red from the cold, his shaggy black hair gleaming in the pale sunlight, the grey eyes alight with quiet pleasure.

'I'm just glad I could find it,' she replied. They started walking towards the house. 'It's been a long time since I last came here.'

They went through the side door into a warm kitchen. Jennie shed her own heavy jacket, draped it over a chair and gazed around the room. It was spotlessly clean and very neat, but without one touch of softness or any attempt at decoration.

'Sit down,' Alex said, motioning her to the square picnic-table by the window. 'I don't have guests very often, so you'll have to forgive the lack of amenities. I'm also not much of a cook, so you'll have to make do with canned soup, which I can just barely heat properly if I follow the directions closely.'

'I'm not a guest, Alex,' she said, sitting down at the table. It was covered with what looked like a flowered cotton flour-sack, clean, but not ironed or even hemmed. 'Remember? I'm here to apply for a job.'

He brought over two steaming bowls of soup, set them down on the table, then went to the cupboard and took out a box of crackers. 'What would you like to drink? Milk? Coffee? Wine?'

'Nothing, thanks. This looks fine.'

'Pretty meagre, I'm afraid,' he said, sitting down on the bench across from her.

'That's all right. I haven't had a terrific appetite lately anyway.'

He eyed her narrowly. 'So I've noticed.'

'Now,' she said brightly, avoiding his comment, 'why don't you tell me just what it is you need? Then you can decide if you think I've had enough experience to fill the job.'

Over lunch they discussed his requirements, which didn't seem to be beyond her ability—merely straightening out his books and keeping track of his accounts, perhaps typing a few business letters and managing his simple filing system.

When they had finished lunch, he took her across the hall to a small office that, in contrast to the kitchen, was in total disarray, with a shabby wooden desk piled high with papers, open folders, ledger sheets and account books. There was an old, green metal filing cabinet in the corner, one drawer half open, its contents spilling out.

'As you can see,' he remarked ruefully, 'I really do need help badly. Your father's office was always in such immaculate shape that I'm certain you can bail me out of the chaos I've created.'

She turned to him with a smile. 'Well, if that's all you need, I don't think it's beyond my powers.'

'Good. That's settled, then.' He led the way into the hall, but instead of heading back towards the kitchen, turned the other way. 'Now I'll show you your quarters.'

She stopped short and stared at his retreating back. 'My quarters?' she asked.

He turned around and gave her a look of surprise. 'Yes. I thought it was all settled. You said you had decided to put the house on the market. You'll need a place to stay. If you're going to work here, it's only logical to move in.'

'I don't know, Alex,' she said dubiously. 'I hadn't really planned on doing that.'

He walked slowly back to her and stood before her, his hands shoved in the back pockets of his trousers, his eyes staring down at the floor. After a few moments, he raised his head and eyed her carefully.

'I'd really like to have you stay out here, Jennie,' he said stiffly. 'I——' He broke off, then cleared his throat and began again. 'I'd appreciate the company, to tell you the truth. I miss your father very much. He was my only real friend in the valley, and now that he's gone. . .' He shrugged helplessly.

'Why, Alex,' she said, 'I thought you preferred it

that way. People leave you alone because you keep so much to yourself.' She grinned. 'In fact, I know two or three ladies in town who would be only too happy to move out here and keep you company.'

He gave her a grim look, half amused, half serious. 'I may get a little lonely at times,' he said with firm conviction, 'but I haven't lost my mind yet.'

Jennie had to laugh. Well, I won't do any match-making for you if you're really determined to remain a bachelor. But I still think it would be better if I stayed with my friend Peggy until I can find a permanent place of my own.'

'I wish you'd reconsider,' he persisted. Then he said softly, 'What is it, Jennie? Are you afraid of gossip?'

She paused, thinking this over. 'No,' she said slowly. 'It's not that.' Still she hesitated.

'Because if you are,' he went on in a joking tone, 'I'll marry you, if you like.'

She gave him a sharp look. He was smiling crookedly at her, and his tone had been light, but there was an undercurrent of seriousness, both in his voice and in the look in his dark grey eyes. Uncertain of his real meaning, she could only stare at him.

To her amazement, a deep reddish flush began to spread from his neck up over his face. 'I didn't mean a real marriage, of course,' he rushed on to explain. 'I have no doubt a new young man will come along for you soon, one who can give you the home and children you want.'

She decided to assume it was a joke, both to cover her own confusion and to help him out. 'Oh, sure,' she said feebly at last. She thought a minute. 'All right,' she said at last with a smile. 'Why not? Live here, I mean,' she amended hastily. 'And I'm not afraid of gossip, so you don't need to go to such extreme measures to help me out. Also,' she added firmly, 'I'll expect you to deduct my board and room from my salary.'

She left soon after that. They'd discussed the details of her move and her employment briefly, and decided that she would move out to his place and start work as soon as she got the house in shape to put on the market.

As she drove back to town, she mulled over the strange conversation and his mind-boggling offer to marry her. Was it a joke? He'd seemed extremely embarrassed the moment the words were out of his mouth. No, she decided, he was only being nice; he only wanted to help out the daughter of his old friend, just as an uncle or older brother would.

Then, suddenly, she recalled the night of the *fiesta* once again. The kiss he had given her then had not been at all brotherly. Although it had been meant to punish her, she had recognised the genuine passion behind it, passion which Alex ordinarily managed to keep entirely bottled up behind that stern façade of his.

Was she being utterly foolish to actually move out there with him, to live under the same roof with this enigmatic man? Then, recalling the years he had come to the house as her father's chess companion, and the careful distance he'd always kept from her, she made up her mind. She had nothing to fear from Alex. Besides, what other choice did she have at this point? If it didn't work out, she could always leave.

* * *

'You're going to *what*?' Peggy exclaimed.

Jennie sighed. 'I'm going to work for Alex Knight out at the winery.'

It was later that evening, and Peggy had come over as planned to help Jennie sort through her father's belongings. They had just cleared out the wardrobe and sorted the clothes into bundles to give away or discard, when Jennie casually told her friend what she planned to do.

'That part I understand,' Peggy said. 'And I think it's great. What I don't get is why you have to *live* with him. I mean, you and he alone out there? What will people think?'

'Oh, come on, Peggy. We won't be alone. He has several men who help him in the fields and at the winery, and a woman who comes in twice a week to clean for him. Besides, it's only Alex. For heaven's sake, he's been like an uncle to me.'

Peggy snorted. 'Some uncle! He's not that much older than we are. He can't be forty yet.'

'He's thirty-seven,' Jennie replied drily. 'OK, more like an older brother, then. But that doesn't mean he's interested in me in that way, or me with him.'

Peggy eyed her suspiciously. 'He's the catch of the whole valley, and you know it.'

Jennie goggled at her. 'Alex?'

'I think he's one of the sexiest men I've ever seen. Don't tell me you've never noticed. That secretive manner he has about him, that marvellous tall, rangy build and those rugged features, the way he lives out there all by himself, his mysterious past. Every single woman in town has been panting to catch his eye ever since he came to Santa Lucia.' Her face fell. 'For all the good it ever did any of us.'

Immediately, his odd proposal that morning jumped into Jennie's mind, and she turned her head away to hide her flushed cheeks. He hadn't really meant it, at least not in that way, and she had no intention of mentioning it to Peggy, who would latch on to it like a dog with a bone and blow it all out of proportion.

'Well, I suppose it's not too late,' she replied evasively. 'Why don't you give it a try?'

'I might just do that,' Peggy said. 'Now that you're going to be living out there, I'll have to come out and visit you from time to time.'

'Fine,' Jennie replied.

They worked in silence for a few more moments, and when Jennie looked up to ask her friend a question she saw that Peggy was eyeing her narrowly, a thoughtful, downright suspicious look on her face.

'Are you sure you're not holding out on me?' she asked.

'What do you mean?' Jennie asked innocently.

'I have the distinct impression there's more going on here than you're telling me.' She shook her head. 'But then, you always were a deep one. I should know by now that if you are hiding something, wild horses won't drag it out of you.'

Jennie held up her right hand and put on her most solemn expression. 'I promise,' she vowed, poker-faced. 'There is nothing going on between Alex Knight and me except what I've told you.' She dropped the hand at her side. 'Honestly, Peggy, he just feels responsible for me because of my father. In fact, I have an idea that he only manufactured that job and offered me a place to live to help me get on my feet again.'

'Well,' Peggy said dubiously. 'If you say so.'

'I do.' It wasn't really a lie. The marriage proposal

had only been a joke, that one far-from-brotherly kiss, months ago, only a form of punishment. 'Now, let's get moving. I promised the estate agent I'd have the house ready to show by next weekend.'

A week later, on a Friday morning, Alex drove into town to help her move. While she waited for him, she walked through the empty house, her footsteps ringing hollowly on the bare wooden floors.

She had packed very little, only her own clothes and personal belongings. All the furniture and household items had been put in storage, and as she wandered around the cold, bare house she had the sense that a chapter was closing in her life.

She'd been born in this house, had grown up in it. It was the only home she'd ever known. Now all that was past, her father gone, Peter out of her life for good. She was an orphan, she thought sadly, and the prospects for creating a new family of her own looked pretty dim at this point.

Then she heard Alex's station-wagon pull into the driveway, breaking into her dismal thoughts. With a firm lift of her chin, she went quickly to the front door to let him in.

'All set to go?' he asked.

'Yes.' She laughed. 'As ready as I'll ever be.'

He eyed her carefully. 'It's a wrench, isn't it, Jennie?'

She nodded. 'But I know it's time.'

She had collected her three suitcases and two cardboard boxes in the hall by the door. Between them, it only took two trips to stow them into the back of the wagon, and in less than half an hour they were on their way to Alex's place.

They drove along in silence. Jennie gazed out of her

window at the passing fields. A few cows were out in a pasture munching on the dried stubble of grass, steam rising from their coats in the chill November air. In one field a brindle Collie dog sat some distance away from a small flock of sheep, watching them with an eagle eye.

'It's rather a barren landscape this time of year,' Jennie commented, just to make conversation.

Alex gave her a quick glance. 'Do you think so?'

'Well, compared to the rest of the year, yes.'

'I rather like it this way.' He had turned his eyes back on the road. 'In fact, there isn't a season here in the valley that doesn't have its particular charms for me. I really like the country, rural life, growing things.' He flashed her a brief smile. 'I find the steady progression of nature quite soothing, in fact.'

'I guess I never thought of it in quite that way,' she said.

'That's because you've always lived here and just take it for granted. You have nothing to compare it with.'

'Such as?'

He shrugged. 'You name it. Try living in any big city for a while, with its jarring noises, everyone rushing around, going nowhere, pushing and shoving to get ahead, to succeed, to be first, and all at someone else's expense. You'd soon realise what a paradise we have here in comparison.'

As he spoke, his voice gradually took on a note of bitterness. Jennie turned to stare at him. His jaw was set, his mouth clamped in a firm line, his eyes fixed on the road ahead, and his large hands gripped the steering-wheel so tightly that the knuckles were white.

To break the tension, she gave an uncertain laugh.

'It sounds as though you have a personal grievance against that world.'

They had reached the turn-off to his ranch by now. He didn't say anything until they were heading down the long drive to the house, but gradually his hands relaxed, the hard lines in his face softened and a faint smile began to play about his mouth.

'Sorry,' he muttered as he parked the station-wagon. 'I didn't mean to blow off like that.' He turned to her. 'There are a lot of things in my past life that I only want to forget, Jennie.' Then he gave a short laugh. 'But obviously I haven't done a very good job of it.'

'Maybe it's better to bring them out in the open,' she said slowly. 'Bottling them up doesn't seem to make them disappear.'

Their eyes met and held. 'You might be right,' he said softly. He smiled at her. 'How in the world did you become so wise at such a tender age?'

'I think that when I lost Peter I did pretty much the same thing. I just couldn't talk about it. Now I realise that it was a mistake to hold it all in the way I did.' She lowered her eyes. 'I guess at the time I didn't want anyone to know how badly I was hurt.'

He reached out a hand and touched her face with just the tips of his fingers, lightly, briefly. 'I knew,' he said gently.

She gave him a sharp look. 'How did you know?'

'Oh, I recognised the signs. Something similar happened to me once, a long time ago. But that's ancient history.' An amused gleam appeared in his eyes. 'Probably before you were born.'

'Oh, Alex!' she cried, stung. 'Don't patronise me that way! I'm not a little girl any more.'

His eyes widened in surprise at her outburst. 'No,'

he said quickly. 'Of course you're not. I'm sorry. I keep forgetting.' He turned and opened his door. 'Come on. We'd better get inside. It's freezing out here.'

They got out of the car and walked together into the house. It was not quite noon. Alex deposited her belongings in the back bedroom that was to be her new home, then started for the door.

'I have several things to attend to before lunch. You probably want to get settled by yourself, anyway. Mrs Anthony is here today. If you need anything, you'll find her in the kitchen. She usually bakes on Friday.'

'I'll be fine,' Jennie said. 'Thanks, Alex.'

When he'd gone, she surveyed her new domain with a critical eye. Like the rest of the house, it was bare, functional, spotlessly clean, and without a trace of warmth or character or any attempt at decoration. There was a narrow wooden bed, chest of drawers, a desk and chair. A shabby patterned carpet covered the floor, and an ancient pair of colourless curtains hung at the window.

Still, it had possibilities. Although it still felt strange to be here at all, and she could hardly think of it was more than a temporary shelter, there was a lot she could do to make it more comfortable and homelike, even during a short visit.

It was a large, well-proportioned room, with plenty of space for more furniture. Depending on how long she decided to stay, or how long Alex wanted her, she might try to fix it up a little, get some of her own things out of storage, make new curtains, even put up some colourful wallpaper and pictures.

There was a spacious walk-in wardrobe on one wall, and next to it a small private bath. She had no idea where Alex slept, but, knowing him, would be willing to bet that it was probably right at the other end of the house.

After unpacking and putting away her things in the wardrobe and chest of drawers and bathroom cabinet, she went down a long hall to the kitchen, where the aroma of fresh baking wafted out in tantalising waves. A stout, elderly, white-haired woman was stooping over the open oven door, examining its contents.

'Mrs Anthony,' Jennie called to her.

The woman closed the oven door carefully, then turned round, wiping her hands on her apron. 'Well, Jennie Corbett!' she exclaimed with a broad smile. 'Welcome. Alex told me you were coming today, and I must say I'm glad to see you.' Then the grin faded and she shook her head sadly. 'I'm so sorry about your father, dear. He'll be sorely missed in these parts.'

'Thank you,' Jennie murmured.

Mrs Anthony brightened. 'But it was a lovely funeral. Such a marvellous turn-out. Everyone loved your dad. Now, how have you been?'

'I'm fine. How about you?'

'Oh, I can't complain. Just a little trouble with sciatica in this cold weather.' Then, with her plump arms akimbo, she examined Jennie minutely through her rimless glasses. 'You look a little thin to me. We'll have to fatten you up.'

Anxious to get busy and make herself useful as soon as possible, Jennie insisted on starting to work that very first afternoon. She soon discovered that Alex's files and accounts were in even worse shape than he'd realised himself.

The small vineyard and family winery he'd purchased

eight years ago had burgeoned and thrived under his careful management, but he'd been so busy during that time expanding his operation and hiring the additional help he'd soon needed that the paperwork had got out of hand and become tangled into a real mess.

Jennie was delighted when she discovered this fact, since it meant that he really did need her help. It was not just charity or loyalty to her father that had moved him to offer her the job, and she pitched in happily, feeling right at home in the world of figures, ledgers, tax forms, and soon found herself handling all his correspondence as well.

Within a week, they had settled into a pleasant routine. Alex was up at dawn, breakfasted alone, then went immediately out to the fields. There was always something that needed doing at a winery. The vines needed pruning or staking or tying or spraying; the rows needed cultivating and weeding; the wine fermenting in the cellar of the vintner house needed checking and testing from time to time.

Jennie arose later, fixed her own breakfast, visited Mrs Anthony if it was one of her days, then went to the small office to tackle the day's work. On rare occasions, she and Alex had a quick lunch together in the kitchen, but most often they didn't meet until the evening meal. In time, Jennie gradually fell into the habit of cooking their dinner herself, just as she had for her father.

In fact, as the weeks went by and November passed into December, her relationship with Alex became so much like the one she'd had with her father that she almost felt as though she were back in her old life. Although his manner was always pleasant and friendly when they did meet, he was a man of few words and rigid self-discipline, who kept himself to a strict routine, and their relationship remained impersonal and businesslike.

Soon it would be Christmas, and as the day approached Jennie became edgy and restless, even slightly depressed. It would be her first Christmas with neither her father nor the warmth and security of Peter's presence in her life, and she wasn't looking forward to it.

Christmas fell on a Friday that year. On the Wednesday morning before, when Jennie went into the kitchen to make her breakfast, she was surprised to see Alex sitting at the table, leafing through the morning paper and drinking coffee. He had on a dress-shirt and tie and was freshly shaven, his dark hair still a little damp from his early morning shower.

'What's the occasion?' she asked as she sat down opposite him.

He glanced up from the paper. 'I have a meeting in town this morning,' he said briefly. 'A group of wine merchants from New York. It seems they were impressed with last year's vintage and are interested in placing an order.'

Mrs Anthony was at the stove, frying bacon. 'I'm making Alex's breakfast,' she called to Jennie. 'Might as well get yours while I'm at it. How do you like your eggs?'

'Oh, thanks, Mrs Anthony,' Jennie replied. 'But please don't bother. I'll just have toast and coffee.'

She started to get up from her chair, but Mrs Anthony made a clucking noise with her tongue and motioned her to stay where she was.

'You sit still. I'll do it.' She turned back to the stove,

muttering under her breath about 'not eating enough
to keep a bird alive' and 'wasting away to nothing'.

Jennie sat back down and gazed out of the window
above Alex's head. A thin crust of frost had formed
during the night, whitening the fields, and the pale
December sun, still low in the eastern sky, glistened on
the sparkling crystals. The kitchen was warm and cosy,
the only sounds to be heard were the bacon sputtering
in the pan and the rustling of the newspaper as Alex
turned the pages.

She glanced at him now. His elbows were propped
on the table, and he was frowning slightly, as though
disagreeing with one of the news items he was reading.
It struck her that he looked very much at home in the
more formal wear, actually quite handsome.

Suddenly she recalled Peggy's comment of some
weeks ago, something about his being one of the sexiest
men she knew. Was Alex sexy? She gave him a closer
look. Unused to thinking of him in those terms, she
couldn't make up her mind.

He certainly was an intensely *masculine* man, all
hard edges and strong features and firm character,
much more so in his way than Peter, who was softer,
more boyish-looking. And, she added, more so than
Mark Doyle, in spite of that young man's macho self-
confidence and predatory instincts.

Mrs Anthony set plates down in front of them,
poured out two more cups of coffee and refilled Alex's
cup, then sat down on the chair between them at the
round table, groaning with the effort, her joints
creaking.

'Well, Alex,' she said when she was finally settled,
'when do you intend to get your tree?'

Alex raised his eyes from the newspaper, a forkful

of food half-way to his mouth, and gave her a puzzled look. 'What tree?'

Mrs Anthony darted a quick look of mute appeal at Jennie, raised her eyebrows and sighed. 'Your Christmas tree!' she said with exaggerated patience.

'Oh, that,' he said dismissively. 'You know I never bother with that kind of nonsense.' He went back to his paper and continued shovelling in his breakfast.

'Well, I never!' Mrs Anthony exclaimed heatedly. 'Christmas without a tree!' She turned to Jennie again. 'How about you? I'll bet *you* want a tree.'

'Not really,' Jennie replied. 'Somehow I can't work up much enthusiasm for Christmas this year.'

Alex glanced at her over his coffee-cup, but didn't say anything, and the rest of the meal was conducted in silence, broken only by Mrs Anthony's heavy breathing and occasional grunts of patent disapproval.

Finally, Alex stood up, drained the last of his coffee, and set the mug down on the table. He reached for his suit jacket, which was hanging on the back of his chair, and slid his arms into it.

'Thanks for the breakfast, Mrs A.,' he said. Then he turned to Jennie. 'Anything I can get you in town?'

'No, thanks, Alex,' she replied. 'I need to make a trip in later myself.'

'Why don't you drive in with me?' He glanced at his watch. 'I can spare a few minutes while you get your coat.'

She shook her head. 'No, you go on ahead. I have some work to clear up around here first.'

Mrs Anthony gave her a stern look. 'Well, now, can't it wait? It's foolish to take two cars.'

'I don't think so,' Jennie persisted. 'I don't want to take you out of your way, Alex.'

'Santa Lucia is not exactly the metropolis of Northern California,' he commented drily. 'Nothing can be too far out of my way. Where do you want to go?'

Jennie glanced down at her hands. 'Actually,' she said in a low voice, 'I was going to the cemetery.'

Alex didn't say anything for several seconds, and Jennie squirmed inwardly, hoping he wouldn't insist on going with her. She wanted to be alone on this visit to her father's grave.

'Sure,' he said at last. 'I understand. Well, I'm off. Wish me luck in my negotiations with the big city wheelers and dealers.'

With that he went out through the kitchen door. In a few moments the station-wagon sputtered into life, and Jennie watched through the window as he drove by.

When Jennie arrived back at the ranch later that afternoon a strange car was parked in front of the house—a sporty little red Corvette. Alex wasn't back yet, so it couldn't be one of his businessmen, and Mrs Anthony's old Ford truck was long gone.

When she got out of the car and started walking up the path to the house, a man got up from the bench on the porch and came towards her. As she neared him, she was startled to see that it was Mark Doyle. Of all people, he was the last person she would have expected ever to meet again.

'Mark!' she called. 'What in the world are you doing here?'

'I came to see you, of course.'

They met on the path, and Jennie smiled up at him, genuinely glad to see him. The visit to her father's grave had been painful, but cathartic, and she felt more light-hearted than she had in weeks—months, even—considering the time she had spent mourning Peter and her lost love.

'Well, I'm flattered,' she said. 'Come inside and I'll make some coffee. It's freezing out here.'

Inside, Mark followed her into the kitchen, both shedding coats as they went, and she waved him to the table. 'Sit down. It'll just take a minute. Is instant all right?'

'Oh, sure. But you don't need to bother.'

'No bother,' she replied, as she put on the kettle and got two mugs out of the cupboard. Actually, she needed a little breathing space to absorb the mere fact of his presence before having to make conversation with him.

'So, how have you been?' she asked, when the coffee was ready and she had sat down across the table from him.

'Great.'

'And how's business?'

'Thriving,' he replied with a grin. Then he sobered. 'Although I miss my visits to your father—and you.'

Jennie set her steaming mug down on top of the table, turning it around in slow circles. She stared silently at it for a moment, then raised her eyes again and smiled at Mark.

'Thanks, Mark,' she said softly. 'It's nice to be missed.'

'Well, now,' he said brusquely, leaning back in his chair and eyeing her thoughtfully. 'What I really came out here for was to see how you were. How is it working out?'

'The job with Alex?' she asked. He nodded. 'It's working out quite well. It came along just when I needed something to keep me busy—and to get me out of that house.'

'What about the—er——' he stumbled. He cleared his throat noisily. 'The living arrangements. I mean, are you and he——' He broke off, reddening.

Jennie threw her head back and laughed. 'Me and Alex? You must be joking. No, believe me. Nothing like that is going on. He and my father were great friends. He's really only doing this as a favour.'

'Well, in that case,' Mark said, brightening, 'how would you like to go out to dinner with me tonight?'

Jennie stared at him. She hadn't expected that, and all she could think of was the last time she and Mark had been together, the night of the dance when he'd virtually forced himself on her. No, she amended. That wasn't true. She'd led him on. She'd had too much to drink, trying to drown her sorrows over Peter's rejection, and had definitely led him to believe that she was willing.

'Why, yes, Mark,' she said at last. 'I'd like that.'

'Good,' he said with satisfaction. 'I have some things to do out this way this afternoon, but I'll come back to pick you up around seven o'clock. Maybe we can drive into Santa Rosa.' He grinned. 'See some real night-life.'

He got up then, and she walked with him to the door. Just as they stepped outside, Alex's station-wagon drove up. He parked in his usual spot, then got out and stood beside it, staring at the two of them standing on the porch together, his eyes narrowed. Then, without changing expression, he started walking slowly towards them.

'Alex,' Jennie said, smiling at him as he approached. 'You remember Mark Doyle?'

There wasn't a hint of an answering smile on Alex's stern features. He stood before them, his hands on his hips, glaring at Mark, who was a good two inches shorter, as though he were some species of dread disease that thretaened to wipe out the grape harvest in the whole valley.

'Doyle,' he said at last with the briefest of nods.

Unnerved by this display of coldness, Jennie began to babble. 'Mark and I are going out to dinner tonight, Alex. We thought we might even drive into Santa Rosa.' She gave a brittle laugh. 'You know, see the sights of the big city——' She broke off lamely as Alex began to stride past Mark towards the house without a word.

When he was inside, and the door had slammed behind him, Mark gave Jennie a puzzled look. 'What the hell was that all about?'

'I have no idea,' Jennie replied slowly. 'Alex isn't exactly the most talkative man I've ever known, but he's usually polite.' Then she brightened. 'Oh, I know. I'll bet his business deal fell through this morning. Poor Alex. He was really counting on it.'

'Tough luck,' Mark said, but not as though he really meant it. 'Well, anyway, I'll see you around seven tonight.'

With a wave, he sauntered over to the car and got inside. As he drove by Jennie waved back at him, then walked slowly into the house, smiling to herself with pleasure at the unexpected invitation.

CHAPTER SIX

THE minute she closed the door behind her, she came face to face with a livid Alex, a current of disapproval emanating from him in almost palpable waves. He was standing directly in her path, his arms crossed over his chest, his face ashen, his grey eyes glittering.

Slowly, Jennie's smile faded, and she gave him a bewildered look. 'Alex?' she said, alarmed. 'What is it?'

Without a word, he raised a hand and took one menacing step towards her. Instinctively she shrank back from him, certain that he intended to strike her. As she gazed up at him in horror, she was hardly able to recognise the Alex she knew in the contorted features of the man standing before her.

'Alex,' she faltered, 'what's happened?'

He was obviously struggling for control, and when he spoke again his tone was strained, but quieter. 'Surely you don't intend to see that guy again?' he said.

So that was it! He was angry because she was going out with Mark Doyle! She could hardly believe it, and as the thought sank in a slow anger began to boil up inside her.

'Now listen, Alex,' she said heatedly. 'Just because you've given me a job and a place to live, it doesn't mean——'

'Are you out of your mind?' he said in a low voice throbbing with emotion. 'Don't you ever learn?'

His face was like thunder now, and, as their eyes

locked together, suddenly she *knew*, in the depths of her being, that at that moment he desired her himself.

Immediately, her anger leaked away. She opened her mouth to speak, but no words came. Her head was whirling crazily. The entire universe had suddenly been turned upside-down. She was struck dumb, immobile, held a prisoner in the glare of those deep grey eyes.

'Alex,' she finally managed to choke out. She took a step towards him and held up a tentative hand. 'Alex, I don't. . .'

Abruptly, he turned away from her, but not before she saw his face go up in flame. He stalked away from her, his hands clenched into fists and held rigidly at his sides. When he reached the bottom of the stairs, he stopped and stood very still for a few seconds.

Jennie didn't know what to do. What did it mean? And how did she feel about it? The memory, even the exact physical sensation, of that one kiss he'd given her so long ago leapt into her mind. She could actually *feel* that mouth burning on hers once again.

Before she could make up her mind whether to rush to his side and fall at his feet, or turn tail and run as fast as her legs would carry her, away from the ranch, away from this tall man's disturbing presence, he had turned round and was smiling crookedly at her.

'OK,' he said, quite calmly now. 'OK, you're right. It's none of my business. I had no right to interfere. I'm not your father, and you're too old for a guardian. I apologise. I just hope you know what you're letting yourself in for.'

Without waiting for a reply, he turned and slowly began to climb the stairs. Jennie stood in the hallway staring up at him. She wanted to call out to him. He couldn't just leave it like that. But what could she say?

Maybe she'd been mistaken. After all, they'd lived in the same house for over a month now, and he'd never by a word or gesture led her to believe that he thought of her in any way except as a young girl, almost a child, who needed his help.

As though by tacit agreement, Jennie and Alex scrupulously managed to avoid each other for the rest of that afternoon, and she didn't see him again all day.

After the scene in the hallway, she had gone into the kitchen to prepare a casserole for the evening meal. Since she was going out to dinner with Mark that night, at least she wouldn't have to face him then.

While she was putting the casserole together, she heard him come downstairs and go out of the back door. Standing back from the window so he wouldn't see her, she watched him go through the gate and down the path that led to the winery. He was dressed in his work clothes—blue jeans, boots, his heavy sheepskin jacket—an ordinary, everyday sight, and one that she had become accustomed to during her stay with him.

Now, however, everything had changed drastically. The thought of Alex Knight as a lover simply boggled her mind. Should she leave the ranch? Wouldn't it be awkward for both of them now to see each other every day, work together, even live in the same house?

At five o'clock, when he usually came back to the house to clean up after work, Jennie went upstairs to her own room, partly in order to avoid Alex, partly because Mark was due at seven. It had been so long since she'd had a real date—since Peter had walked out of her life—that she wanted to give herself plenty of time to get ready for it.

After soaking for half an hour in a hot bath until the water was cold, she dried off and surveyed her wardrobe, a depressing sight. Every dress reminded her of Peter; the cherry-red wool he used to say brought colour to her cheeks, the pale sea-green silk that he'd told her matched the colour of her eyes, the sophisticated black she'd worn the night they'd set their wedding date.

She finally decided on the black. Although her father would hate the idea, she was still officially in mourning for him. Her mother's pearl necklace and earrings would make it a little more festive.

As she dressed, the dark mood generated by those reminders of Peter gradually lifted, and by the time she went into the bathroom to comb her hair and put on her make-up, she was feeling oddly rather pleased with herself.

She smiled at her reflection in the mirror. She had a dinner date with an attractive man, her old longing for Peter seemed to be less intense and long lasting, and, if she was correct in her interpretation, another attractive man had just that afternoon shown signs of finding her desirable. In just six months, she'd gone from being jilted to being sought after, and that made up for a lot of the old hurt.

At the last minute, she changed her mind about the black dress and hurriedly exchanged it for the cherry-red wool. She had something to celebrate, after all.

By a quarter to seven, she was ready. After one last quick glance in the mirror she ran downstairs to wait for Mark. She didn't want to have to witness another sticky encounter between him and Alex, who was nowhere to be seen anyway.

In a few minutes she heard Mark's car approach up

the long driveway. She grabbed her coat and bag and opened the door to wait for hum out on the porch, just in case Alex decided to put in a appearance after all.

It was then that she noticed that his station-wagon wasn't parked in its usual spot. He must have driven off while she was running her bath or drying her hair and she hadn't heard him.

Where could he have gone? Alex rarely went out at night, and when he did he always told her where he was going and when he'd be back, so that she would be able to get hold of him if she needed him. She wondered now for the first time if the reason he stayed at home so much was because he didn't like to leave her alone in the house at night.

Then she heard Mark's car door slam, and he came walking towards her. 'Ah!' he called. 'A prompt woman! Are you ready to go?'

Jennie had prepared herself to spend at least part of the evening fending off Mark's advances. To her surprise, he didn't once get out of line or even make one of his usual suggestive remarks. In fact, throughout the whole time they spent together, he treated her with an elaborate courtesy that was almost comical—possibly, she thought later, in deference to her recent bereavement.

In any case, by the time dinner was half over she'd realised that she was having a very good time. She felt relaxed and at ease with him. He was a good-looking man, too, with his flaming auburn hair, stocky muscular build and confident air.

At the same time, however, she also found herself occasionally staring off into space, distracted momentarily by thoughts of the scene with Alex that afternoon. It seemed rather remote to her now, in the busy restaurant, with the dim lighting, the soft music playing in the background, the low him of conversation and the delicious smells. Still, she couldn't quite get it out of her mind. It was like a puzzle she had been set to solve, and there seemed to be several pieces missing.

'Hey,' Mark said to her at one point. 'Where are you?'

She stared at him. 'I'm right here,' she replied. 'Sitting across from you.'

'It looked to me as though you were a million miles away,' he commented drily. 'Something on your mind?'

She smiled at him. 'Not really,' she hedged. She took a mouthful of lasagne. 'This is wonderful, Mark. I've never been here before. Is it new?'

He nodded. They had decided to drive into Santa Rosa, a much larger town than Santa Lucia, with more to offer in the way of good dining, and he'd brought her to a small Italian restaurant on the outskirts of town.

'Here,' he said, 'have some more wine.' He raised the carafe and topped her glass. 'Now, out with it, Jennie. Something's bugging you. Are you sorry you came?' He flushed slightly. 'I mean, if you're worried that I'm going to make a pass at you——'

'No, of course not. Don't mind me. It's just my way.' She laughed lightly. 'I distract easily. Does it bother you?'

'Not unless it's some other guy who's doing the distracting,' he replied in a joking tone. Then his face sobered. 'Is it still Peter?'

Jennie shook her head. 'No. That's over and done with, and I came to terms with it long ago. I don't know. So much has happened to me in the past few months, I haven't quite caught up with it.'

'You still miss your father, don't you?'

'Yes. Yes, I do,' she replied softly.

'Well, if I read Doc Corbett right, the last thing he would have wanted was for you to grieve for him. He was a great believer in life for the living.'

'You're right. And I am trying.'

'Good.' He leaned across the table towards her. 'Don't take this wrong, Jennie,' he said in a low voice. 'It's not a pass. But you look great in that red dress— downright gorgeous, in fact. It puts colour in your cheeks.'

Jennie choked on her wine in an effort to stifle the laughter that bubbled up at his words, which were almost exactly the same as those Peter used to say. Somehow, though, coming from Mark they only seemed funny. It occurred to her out of the blue that you would never catch Alex saying a thing like that, and she caught herself, sobering instantly.

What had made her think of that? And what made Alex so different from both Mark and Peter? Was it only that he was so much older? Peter was only twenty-seven, but Mark had to be in his early thirties, not that much difference.

Then she realised that Mark was staring curiously at her again. She dismissed her wayward thoughts, put on her brightest smile and gave him her whole attention for the rest of the evening.

From that night on, Jennie's relationship with Alex changed in subtle but definite ways. They seemed to be walking on eggshells, treating each other with elaborate courtesy whenever they met, and the distance between them widened further with each passing day.

Christmas came and went virtually unnoticed, much

to Mrs Anthony's disgust, except for one small incident.

On Christmas Eve, Jennie was in the kitchen glumly washing up the dishes from the late supper that Mrs Anthony had left for them, and feeling very sorry for herself. On this, her first Christmas without her father, her spirits had sunk to their lowest ebb since his death, and she'd deliberately spent the whole day virtually chained to her desk, working on Alex's year-end books, in the hope of tiring herself out so that she could sleep the depressing night away.

As soon as she'd finished the washing-up, she turned out the light in the kitchen and started off down the hall towards her bedroom. As usual, Alex had disappeared after supper, but as she passed by the living-room she could see a light burning inside, and she saw that he was sitting in front of a crackling fire, leafing through the newspaper. On the coffee-table by the couch was a bottle of wine and, she noticed, two glasses. Was he expecting company?

As she stood hesitating in the doorway, he looked up from his newspaper and smiled at her. 'Ah, Jennie, there you are. If you're through, why don't you come in and have a Christmas drink with me? It's pleasant here by the fire.'

In the firelight the normally bleak room looked warm and cosy, and, in spite of their recent coolness, Alex *was* another human being, and it *was* Christmas, after all. The least she could do was share a bottle of wine with him.

'All right,' she replied, stepping inside. 'Then we can tell Mrs Anthony we did do *some* celebrating.'

She sat down beside him and watched while he

poured out the wine. He handed her a glass, then raised his in the air. 'Cheers,' he said.

'Cheers,' she murmured in reply, feeling anything but cheerful.

They drank in silence for a while, and soon the delicious wine, one of Alex's best vintages, and the warmth from the brightly glowing fire began to make her feel better. Things weren't so bad. She had a roof over her head, a job, a little money in the bank. She settled back on the couch and closed her eyes.

She was just about to drift off when she heard Alex clear his throat loudly. 'Er, Jennie.'

She turned to him and saw with some surprise that he had a small oblong box in his hand, along with a rather sheepish expression on his face.

'Merry Christmas, Jennie,' he said, holding the box out to her.

'Why, Alex,' she said, 'I had no idea you were even thinking of exchanging gifts. I'm afraid I don't have anything for you. You seemed so adamant about ignoring Christmas that I didn't even——'

He waved a hand in the air. 'Never mind. Don't worry about that. Why don't you open it? If you don't like it, I'm sure we can exchange it.'

Hastily, she unwrapped the package and lifted the lid of a dark blue velvet box. Inside was a thin gold chain with a lovely cameo strung on it, delicately carved and obviously antique. She lifted it carefully out of the box and gazed wide-eyed at Alex, who was staring intently at her.

'Alex, it's beautiful,' she breathed. 'I love it.'

'Well, that's all right, then,' he said, clearly greatly relieved. 'I thought you might, but one never knows.

The chain is new, but the cameo belonged to my mother—and to her mother before her.'

'Why, Alex, I'm really very touched. Thank you so much.' She cocked her head to one side and gave him a mischievous grin. 'Although somehow it's hard to think of you having a mother.'

'Oh, yes. I had a very wonderful mother, as a matter of fact. I was only a kid when she died, but she was a great loss.' A sudden, dark frown clouded his face. 'In a way, though, I'm almost grateful that she didn't live to see——' His voice broke off abruptly, and he turned to stare intently into the flames.

'To see what?' Jennie asked slowly.

He shrugged. 'Oh, a lot of things happened that would have made her unhappy. But let's not go into that. I'm just glad you like it.'

Although she was longing for him to go on, to open up to her about his past, her instinct warned her that he had already gone further than he'd intended. She held up the cameo to admire it.

'Alex, I don't feel quite right about taking this. Since it's so important to you, wouldn't you rather save it for someone else?'

He gave her a puzzled look. 'Someone else? Who did you have in mind? I can't think of anyone else I'd rather see wearing it.'

'Well, you're not exactly ancient, you know,' she said in a teasing tone. 'You could marry, maybe have a daughter you'd like to give it to some day.'

He shook his head vigorously. 'No. That's not on the cards for me. Besides, I want you to have it. I know I don't always show it,' he went on slowly, 'but it's meant a lot to me, your being here the past few months.'

'Glad I could help you out,' she said lightly. 'I think

the office is running pretty smoothly, if I do say so myself.'

He shook his head. 'I wasn't talking about the office. It's you. You've been like a breath of fresh air, given new life to a place that was dead before you came.' He ducked his head and reached for the bottle of wine. 'Well, enough of that,' he said gruffly. 'Let's have one more, for Mrs Anthony's sake.'

When he had refilled her glass, Jennie raised it in a toast of her own. 'To Mrs Anthony,' she said solemnly.

Alex clinked his glass against hers. 'To Mrs Anthony,' he repeated.

In late February the valley enjoyed an early warm spell, a harbinger of the spring that was just around the corner. Although Jennie wore the cameo and chain almost constantly, Alex never remarked on it, nor did he ever refer to the conversation they'd had on Christmas Eve, and before long the pleasant intimacy they'd enjoyed that night began to seem like a dream to her.

Even so, on one or two brief occasions she did catch him staring fixedly at her, an oddly intense expression on his face. But when their eyes met fleetingly, and she gave him a questioning glance, hoping he would tell her what was on his mind, he always looked away.

By now, Jennie had Alex's files and accounts organised and was conducting most of the business correspondence by herself, only seeking his advice when a serious policy decision had to be made. With all the office affairs in such good order, she had a lot more free time, and under the spell of the sudden balmy weather she found herself growing restless.

She was also lonely. Alex was no company, Mrs Anthony only came twice a week, and since Mark had all the other nearby towns in his sales territory to cover besides Santa Lucia he was only in town for a few days at a time. And she hadn't had a good visit with Peggy for weeks.

One Wednesday evening when she and Alex were eating one of their largely silent dinners, Jennie decided to tackle him on the subject. After the way he had reacted to her first date with Mark and his stern silence ever since, she wasn't sure how he would react to *any* suggestion that involved her friends.

He sat across from her, immersed in one of his endless nursery catalogues, and when she cleared her throat loudly he glanced up at her, frowning slightly.

'Alex, would it be all right if I invited my friend Peggy out here for dinner on Saturday night?'

He gazed blankly at her for a moment, then said, 'Of course. Why do you even ask? This is your home, too, you know.'

She stoutly resisted the temptation to remind him of the near-tantrum he'd had when Mark had first showed up, and was about to thank him when he continued speaking.

'I'll just have an early supper on my own that night,' he said, 'so you can be alone with your friend.'

'You don't have to do that,' she protested. 'That isn't at all what I had in mind. I'd like to have you eat with us, and I know Peggy would, too. I thought I'd fix something really special.' She laughed. 'Maybe get some tips from Mrs Anthony the next time she comes. Please say you'll join us.'

'We'll see,' he replied. He was silent for a moment, then, raising his hand in a diffident, offhand gesture, he went on in a low voice. 'Jennie,' he said, 'it distresses me that you felt you had to ask my permission to invite your friend for dinner. And it occurs to me that I never did apologise to you for the way I behaved the night Mark Doyle showed up here.'

'You don't need to, Alex,' she said quickly. 'I understand.'

'Do you?' He sighed and gave her a searching look. 'I doubt it, but that's neither here nor there. Let's just say I had serious reservations about him after his performance at the *fiesta* last summer.' He smiled wryly. 'I guess I still think of you as a young girl who needs protection.'

'Not that young, Alex,' she said tartly. It annoyed her that he insisted on treating her like a child. 'I'll be twenty-four soon, a grown woman. Besides, if it'll make you feel any better, I should tell you that Mark has behaved like a perfect gentleman on all our dates. We both had a little too much to drink that night of the dance, and what happened was as much my fault as it was his.'

She had to smile at the wave of sheer relief that washed over his face. He really took his role as surrogate father seriously, and the realisation made her warm to him. She was also intensely grateful that they seemed to be back on their old comfortable footing at last. For the first time in weeks they'd actually had a friendly conversation.

They continued eating in silence after that, and when Alex had finished he rose to his feet and started for the stairs, as he usually did. At the door he stopped for a moment, then turned around and slowly retraced his steps until he was standing beside her chair, looking down at her.

'You've been here for three months now, Jennie,' he

said. 'And, while I'm grateful for the way you've shaped up my chaotic business affairs, I wonder if you've given any thought to your future. What I mean to say,' he added quickly, 'is that you can stay here forever as far as I'm concerned, but it's been on my mind lately that it can't be a very exciting life for you.'

Jennie looked up at him. 'If you know me at all, Alex,' she said slowly, 'you should realise that excitement isn't one of my ambitions. I'm comfortable here. I like the work. If you want me to stay, I will, at least until. . .'

'Until the right young man comes along?' he asked with a slow smile.

'Well, yes, I suppose so.'

'Then I take it you haven't given any more thought to continuing your education.'

She frowned. 'That's just not on the cards for me, Alex. For better or worse, I'm stuck with myself, with who I am. All I ever wanted was a home, a family. I just wasn't cut out to be a career woman.'

'Well, I could be wrong about Mark. Maybe he'll be the one who can give you what you really want. I hope so, for your sake, but I have to admit that I still have my doubts.'

She was about to reassure him that, much as she liked Mark and enjoyed his company, she knew in her heart that he wasn't the one. But something stopped her. For some reason, she didn't want Alex to feel too smug about her relationship with Mark. Keeping him in suspense about that gave her a pleasant sense of power over this man who seemed so strong and invulnerable.

* * *

That Saturday night, everything seemed to go wrong. Jennie's first mistake was her decision to serve dinner in the dining-room, a draughty, musty-smelling room off the front parlour that was never used. It had turned suddenly cold that day, and Jennie sat at the table freezing in her green silk dress.

She had placed Alex at the head, with Peggy at the side, which was her second mistake, since from the moment they all sat down Peggy's chair inched closer and closer to Alex, leaving Jennie sitting at the foot of the table, literally out in the cold, regarding both temperature and conversation.

Then the cheese and mushroom soufflé had fallen dramatically after she'd peered in the oven at it once too often. The salad wasn't bad, and Mrs Anthony's buttery rolls filled in the gap nicely, but by the time Jennie served the lumpy chocolate mousse that she'd prepared for dessert she was almost in tears.

She sat down in her limbo at the foot of the table, gazing miserably at her two companions, who by now were almost side by side at the other end. Peggy had hardly addressed one word to her throughout the whole evening, except to advise her to beat the mousse more thoroughly next time before cooling it, and for heaven's sake to keep her head out of the oven when a soufflé was rising.

Since Peggy was an even worse cook than she was, these titbits of culinary advice were not well received, but she couldn't very well give voice to the tart reply that rose to her lips—not so long as Alex was present. What she regretted most of all, by the time she served the coffee, was that she had invited him to join them in the first place.

Peggy was leaning an elbow on the table, her chin

cupped in her hand, gazing at Alex in undisguised fascination. 'And the buyers from New York actually offered you a higher price for your vintage than you intended to ask? That's amazing, Alex. As a buyer myself, I can assure you that such a thing isn't done unless the seller comes across as an astute businessman. You must have impressed them.'

Alex seemed to be basking in this outrageous display of ego-stroking, lapping it up as though he believed every word of it. He looked very handsome tonight, Jennie had to admit. He was wearing a crisp white dress-shirt, a dark suit and tie, and he laughed and smiled more in that one evening than Jennie had seen him do in all the time she'd known him.

She sat there glaring at them both. She was cold, her dinner had failed miserably, and now here was her best friend openly flirting with *her* Alex.

My Alex? she asked herself. What made me think that? She didn't own him, after all. She began to calm down as she recalled that Peggy had always been interested in him. Why not give her this shot at him, if that was what she wanted?

Finally the disgusting meal was over. Alex set his napkin down beside his plate and rose to his feet. He looked down the table at Jennie, a gently mocking smile on his lips.

'That was an—um—interesting dinner, Jennie,' he said. 'Thank you for inviting me.' He turned to Peggy. 'It was nice to see you again, Peggy. You must come out here more often.'

'Oh, I will,' Peggy breathed, gazing up at him adoringly.

'Now,' Alex sent on, 'I'll leave you two ladies to talk in private. I have an appointment in town.'

Peggy's face fell and she opened her mouth to protest. Obviously thinking better of it, she only said, 'Thanks for the invitation, Alex. I just might take you up on it.'

With another brief smile, Alex turned and walked out of the room. When he was gone the two girls didn't look at each other or utter a word until they heard him go out of the front door and start up the engine of his car.

Then Peggy turned swiftly to Jennie. 'I wonder what his appointment in town could be?'

Jennie shrugged. 'I'm afraid I'm not up on Alex's personal life. As a matter of fact, I didn't even know he had one. We both keep pretty much to ourselves out here. Strictly business.'

She started clearing the table, and after a moment Peggy got up to help her. Neither of them said anything more until they'd finished and were in the nice *warm* kitchen, washing up. Then, after Peggy had put the last dish in the cupboard, she turned to Jennie, who was wiping off the draining-board.

'Er, Jennie,' she began hesitantly. 'Do you think I came on too strong with Alex tonight?'

Jennie ducked her head to hide a smile. 'I don't know, Peggy,' she said in a serious tone. 'You weren't exactly subtle, but it's possible that some men might like the more direct approach.' She gave her friend a twisted smile. 'But, with my track record, I'm probably the last one in the world to ask for advice about men.'

Peggy hung the tea-towel on the rack beneath the sink, biting her lip and frowning thoughtfully, as though trying to make up her mind about something. Then she turned and gave Jennie a direct look.

'I saw Peter the other day,' she stated flatly.

'Oh?' Jennie continued scrubbing the spotless counter-top. 'How is Peter?' She couldn't quite hide the edge in her voice.

'He asked about you.'

'Really? How thoughtful of him!'

'I don't know for sure,' Peggy went on, 'but I got the impression that he still cares about you.'

Jennie threw her head back and laughed. 'Oh, come on, Peggy! If Peter feels anything at all, it's only guilt.'

Peggy shrugged. 'You're probably right. What a rat he turned out to be.'

'Oh, well. As everyone told me at the time, better to find that out now instead of after we were married.'

Peggy glanced at her watch. 'It's getting late. I'd better go.' She grinned. 'Thanks for the dinner.'

Jennie winced, and they started walking together out into the hall, where Peggy retrieved her coat. At the front door, she turned to Jennie and gave her a tentative, almost shamefaced look.

'Can I ask you a personal question?'

'Sure.'

'Is there anything going on between you and Alex?'

Jennie's eyes widened, and she shook her head vigorously. 'No, of course not. What makes you think that?'

'Oh, I don't know. Just the way he looks at you sometimes. You know that hungry look men get.'

Jennie laughed as she opened the door. 'No, as a matter of fact, I don't. Men don't seem to think of me that way.' She sighed. 'Even Mark Doyle has barely laid a hand on me. Guess I'm just not any man's idea of a sex symbol.'

* * *

Late that night, Jennie was awakened out of a light, restless sleep by a noise coming from the direction of the kitchen. Groggily she glanced at the clock on the bedside table. In the light of the bright moon shining through her window, she saw that it was past two o'clock.

The noise came again. It must be Alex, she thought, but just in case she slipped out of bed and went to the window to make sure his station-wagon was in its usual spot in the driveway. As she pulled aside the curtain and peered out into the darkness, her heart skipped a beat. It wasn't there. He hadn't come home yet!

Whoever it was out in the kitchen, it couldn't be Alex! Her heart started pounding. What should she do? Call the police? But she didn't have a telephone in her bedroom. Go back to bed and hope he would go away?

Finally, she decided that she simply had to at least investigate. As quietly as possible, she tiptoed barefoot out into the hall. Keeping close to the wall, she crept slowly towards the kitchen, where a dim light was burning. The sounds were growing louder now. She could hear water running, the clink of a glass.

Drawn now almost against her will, she continued on until she reached a point where she was in the shadows but could see into the kitchen. She could still see very little, however, so she took one more cautious step. Then she stopped short in her tracks and stared.

Standing at the kitchen sink was Alex. He was half turned away from her, his head tilted up, drinking a glass of water. He was wearing only a pair of dark trousers, leaving his upper body bare, and in the glow of the light over the sink the long, ugly scar on his smooth chest was plainly visible.

She stood there in the shadows staring at him, transfixed by the sight of the strong, lithe body, the broad shoulders and muscled chest, tapering down to a narrow waist and slim hips under the low-slung dark trousers. She watched the workings of his long throat as he swallowed, the way his dark hair grew on the back of his neck, a little too long, as usual.

Without thinking, she took a step forwards. Her bare toe came up against something hard, and she gave a little cry of pain. To her dismay, Alex immediately whirled around and came walking out of the kitchen directly towards her.

'Who's there?' he called in a low voice. 'Is that you, Jennie?'

It was too late to turn and run back to the safety of her own bedroom. She might as well brazen it out now that she'd been caught. Still wincing from the pain of her stubbed toe, she hurried forwards to meet him.

'Yes, it's only me.' He was standing in the doorway now, and she had come up to within only a few steps away from him. 'I heard a noise in here, and when I didn't see your car in the driveway I thought I'd better take a look.'

'I had car trouble in town and caught a lift home.' His voice sounded low, almost hollow, as though it were coming across a deep chasm from a far distance.

His tall form was outlined against the light of the kitchen, his face in shadow, but she could still make out the slight scowl on his face and grasp the fact that he was staring at her fixedly. They stood like that for a few moments, until suddenly he reached behind him to grab his shirt, which was hanging on the back of a chair.

'Don't,' she said quickly. Impelled almost against

her will, she walked quickly towards him, covering the few steps that separated them. 'Please, don't.'

She stood before him now, staring hypnotically at the livid scar. Then, as though in a trance, she reached out and ran her fingers lightly along the angry, puckered ridge, from his shoulder down across his powerful chest muscles, to the very edge of his wide belt. As her fingers touched his skin, she could feel the muscles quivering underneath.

'You never did tell me where you got this,' she said.

'It was in the war,' he said in a muffled voice. 'Vietnam. I got in the way of a swinging machete.'

Slowly she raised her eyes to his. He was staring down at her with an undisguised open hunger that took her breath away. At the same time she realised that she was standing there clad only in her short cotton nightgown. Somehow it didn't seem important, and she boldly met his gaze, searching the deep grey eyes for some sign, some indication of what would happen next.

For a second he hesitated. Then, making a low kind of growl deep in his throat, he dropped the shirt on the floor and reached out for her. With a little cry she fell towards him, and the next thing she knew she was enclosed within a pair of strong arms, cradled close to his broad, bare chest.

'Ah, Jennie,' he murmured at her ear. 'My little Jennie.'

She could feel the thudding of his heart next to her own, his hot, laboured breathing at her ear. He held her tightly, pressing his body against hers with a sense of such urgency, such intensity that she responded eagerly, mindlessly to his own powerful need.

Then, with his rough cheek rasping against hers, his large hands clutching at her shoulders, her waist, her hips, his mouth came down on hers, searing her very soul with a long, open-mouthed kiss. Feeling as though she were drowning, she instinctively raised her arms up around his neck, returning his hot kiss with a sudden powerful need of her own.

When he finally tore his mouth away from hers and pulled his head back, she still clung to him, digging her fingers into the smooth, hard flesh of his shoulders, nestling her head against his chest, her lips on the scar.

It flashed into her head that nothing in her whole life had ever made her happier or felt so right to her as being held in Alex's arms. She was by no means certain how this had all come about, but she could think about that later. Right now, however, she wanted him, all of him, and was ready to give him whatever he asked of her.

She raised her head, eager to tell him what was on her mind and in her heart, but when she saw the look on his face, dark with pain, a cold chill ran up her spine. At the same time, he grasped her roughly by the shoulders and held her away from him.

'Hell, I'm sorry, Jennie,' he said, his chest still heaving with his laboured breathing.

'Alex, it's all right,' she said.

She reached out blindly for him, but his arm shot out immediately to grasp her hand, forestalling her, pushing her back even further away from him. His eyes were cold with fury, his lips curled in contempt.

'This is what happens,' he ground out roughly, 'when little girls go parading around in their nightgowns in the middle of the night. You'd better get back to bed before things really get out of hand.' His mouth quirked in a parody of a smile. 'I'm only a man, Jennie.

If you know what's good for you, you'll keep that in mind from now on.'

Without giving her a chance to reply, he reached down to pick up the shirt he had dropped, and slipped it on. Then he turned away from her and slowly began to button it.

CHAPTER SEVEN

IF HE had thrown a bucket of iced water on her, Jennie couldn't have been more shocked. Totally confused, she went hot, then so cold that her teeth chattered.

Her first instinct was to reach out to him, to demand an explanation, to beg him not to send her away, to tell him that it was all right for him to want her, that she wanted him, too. But that hard, stern back was like a stone wall shutting her out, inexorable and final.

With a little cry, she turned on her heel and ran down the hall to the safety of her own room. Flinging herself on the bed, she lay there, her eyes squeezed tight, as the hot waves of shame washed over her.

What had made him pull away from her in that way? She couldn't possibly have been mistaken about his desire for her. Passion had shone from his eyes, was apparent in his whole body, the way he had clung to her, that one long burning kiss. And it couldn't just be because of the difference in their ages. Genuine desire transcended age, and, besides, it wasn't that great.

All she could think of was that she had been rejected once again. First Peter, now Alex. What was wrong with her? Was there some kind of malignant curse on her that the only two men she'd ever really been attracted to had ended up leaving her?

She tossed and turned during the small hours of the night, going over it again and again. Finally, further than ever from any plausible conclusion, towards morning she fell into an exhausted sleep.

* * *

123

When she awoke, the sun was shining through her bedroom window, and the birds were singing in the trees. Opening one eye, she glanced at the bedside clock and saw that it was a quarter past ten.

As the events of the previous night flooded into her dulled brain, she sat bolt upright in bed, suddenly filled with certainty. The first thing she had to do was get away from here. She couldn't possibly stay at the ranch another day now. And, after last night, he probably wouldn't want her to. She would leave today.

She stumbled out of bed and peered out of the window. There was no sign of Alex or his car. It was Sunday. Maybe he'd slept late, too. She padded over to the door, opened it a crack and listened intently.

Not a sound was to be heard. The house was utterly silent. Then she remembered that Alex had left his car in town. Maybe someone had come out to pick him up while she'd been asleep. If she hurried, she might be able to pack a few things and get out before he returned. She could stay with Peggy for a while until she decided what to do.

She threw on some clothes, then, with every muscle tense, she crept slowly and stealthily down the hall, stopping and listening at every step, just in case.

By the time she reached the kitchen, there was still no sign of Alex, and, breathing a little more easily, she stepped inside. It could be a long day, and she'd better get some food inside her while she had the chance.

The first thing she saw was the note. It was taped to the door of the refrigerator, a piece of scrap paper, hurriedly torn, covered in black ink with Alex's slashing, upright handwriting.

'Jennie,' it said. 'Had to leave this morning for New

York on business. Forgot to tell you last night. Will be back next Sunday.'

Brief and to the point, it was signed simply, 'Alex.'

Well, that settled that. He was gone. There was no hurry. She had the rest of the week to pack and get his pending business affairs up to date. Then she would leave *him* a note, equally terse, and be long gone by the time he got back.

Filled with renewed determination, she spent the rest of the day getting her clothes in order. She found that keeping busy calmed her down, but as she washed and ironed and mended she couldn't help dwelling on that strange scene with Alex, or trying to understand it.

By evening her entire wardrobe was in shape, everything clean and folded neatly. Worn out, she fell into bed at nine o'clock, no closer to understanding Alex Knight than she'd been that morning.

Monday was one of Mrs Anthony's 'days', and as usual she was in the kitchen when Jennie came in for breakfast, a fresh pot of coffee perking on the stove, the smell of baking in the air.

'Good morning, Jennie,' she called cheerfully. 'Where's Alex? He's usually here waiting for his breakfast when I arrive.'

'Oh, he had to go to New York on business,' Jennie replied. She poured herself a cup of coffee and sat down at the table. 'I think he's probably going to meet with those wine merchants who were in town last week.'

'Sounds like it might be a big order,' Mrs Anthony said with satisfaction.

'Could be.'

'When will he be back?'

'Not until Sunday.'

Jennie wondered if she should mention the fact that she'd be leaving the ranch this week. Not yet, she decided. No point in getting involved in a lot of explanations just yet. Besides, she still wasn't quite sure what she was going to do.

He *had* wanted her. There wasn't a doubt in her mind about that. Then what had changed his mind? The more she thought about it, the less plausible the age difference explanation seemed to her. There had to be something more to it than that. Another woman, perhaps. Maybe even a wife!

'Mrs Anthony,' she said.

'Yes, dear?'

'You've known Alex a long time, haven't you?'

'Ever since he arrived in Santa Lucia and bought this place.'

'Do you know anything about his life before he came here?'

Mrs Anthony turned around and gave her a searching look. 'No, I don't,' she said brusquely. 'And if you know Alex at all, you surely realise that he's one man who never talks about himself.'

'I wonder why he's so secretive about his past. I mean, why make such a mystery of it? There must be something he doesn't want anyone to know about.'

Mrs Anthony drew herself up stiffly to her full five feet. 'Now, Jennie,' she said sternly. 'Alex is not a boy. He undoubtedly does have a past of some kind, but if you're saying there might be something shady about it——' She broke off and clucked disapprovingly.

'Oh, no. Nothing like that,' Jennie quickly explained. 'I guess I was thinking more about his personal life. For example, I wonder if he's ever been married, had children?'

'Well, I don't know for sure, of course, but I've worked for him almost eight years now, and if there was a wife and family in the background I can't imagine that I wouldn't have heard something about them by now.'

It was on the tip of Jennie's tongue to mention the scar, but something made her hesitate. He'd said he'd been wounded in combat. Why would he lie?

She'd finished her light breakfast by now, anyway, and Mrs Anthony was getting out the mop and bucket to scrub the kitchen floor, a task which she attacked so whole-heartedly that Jennie knew from experience there would be no more conversation until she was finished.

Slowly she got up from the table and went out into the hall, feeling a little at a loose end. For some reason, this morning she wasn't quite so eager to leave. The urgency that had impelled her to rush around in a frenzy yesterday and get all her clothes in order so that she could pack and get out immediately seemed to have petered out.

There was really no hurry. He would be gone all week. She didn't have to leave immediately. Besides, she needed to make sure the office was tidied up, and bring Alex's accounts and correspondence up to date. In spite of that brutal rejection, he had been kind to her after her father had died, and she owed him that much. She couldn't really hate him. She just didn't understand him.

On her way to the office, she passed by the back door. Mrs Anthony had opened it to air the house, and, glancing through it at the rolling hills and blue sky, Jennie decided to take one last, short stroll outside. The office work wouldn't take long. It could wait another half an hour.

The slight breeze coming in through the doorway was quite warm. She wouldn't even need a sweater. She stepped outside and drew in a deep breath of the sweetly scented air.

Spring came early to the valley, and even now, in late February, the flowering quince by the side of the house was showing a hint of bright orange in its swelling buds. Tender new leaves were beginning to sprout on the gnarled branches of the grapevines, casting a light green haze over the fields.

As Jennie wandered around from one familiar spot to another—the brick building that housed the winery in the distance, the tall, spreading pepper tree by the driveway, the small pond beside it glistening in the early morning sunshine, the fresh clean air, balmy on her bare arms and face—it struck her how much she had come to love this place and how sorry she would be to leave it.

Was it possible, she wondered, picking at a blade of grass, that the ugly episode of Saturday night could be forgotten, that perhaps when Alex came back it would simply be buried, never referred to again, and she could stay after all?

Then she saw again the look in his eyes when he had pushed her away, stony, forbidding, angry, and hot waves of humiliation and shame filled her all over again. She would never forget that, never in a million years. How could she face him again after that?

She trudged slowly back inside and down the hallway to the small office at the back of the house where she did her work. Mrs Anthony was humming in the kitchen, and from the distance a tractor sputtered into life. Otherwise, the house was silent.

She sat at her desk working for the next two hours, and when she finally raised her weary head from the last week's ledger sheet, rubbing a hand over the back of her neck and flexing her cramped fingers, her eye fell on the small steel safe in the corner of the room where Alex kept his ready cash.

Ordinarily, he was the only one who ever opened it, but if she was going to do a thorough job she should make an accounting of the actual cash he had on hand. He'd given her the combination. There was no reason why she shouldn't open it herself. In fact, Alex left it unlocked most of the time.

She found the slip of paper on which he'd written the combination in the top drawer of the desk, then got up and went over to the safe. Stooping down, she twirled the lock to the appropriate numbers, unhooked it and opened the heavy steel door.

Inside was a green metal strongbox where the cash was kept. She pulled it out and looked inside. There was quite a bit of money there—much more than the couple of hundred dollars that Alex liked to keep on hand. Some of it really should be banked.

She was just about to rise to her feet and carry the strongbox over to the desk to make an accurate count when her eye fell on another box, pushed far back inside. Thinking there might be more cash inside, she pulled it out, too, and set them both on the desk.

The other box was smaller and made of polished wood with brass hinges and fittings. There was a small lock, but when she pressed the catch the lid sprang up immediately. Inside was a bundle of letters tied

together with string, and beneath it a small manila
envolope, unsealed, which might possibly contain cash.

Setting aside the letters, she opened the envelope,
felt inside and pulled out what looked like a stack of
photographs loosely wrapped in tissue-paper. She
stared down at the pile of letters sitting on top of the
desk, then at the pictures she held in her hand.

At that moment, she was faced with a critical decision. She knew the right thing to do was to stuff
everything back in the box and replace it in the safe.
There was certainly no money here, and that was what
she'd been looking for. She hesitated. While she
wouldn't dream of reading the letters, it couldn't hurt
anything to take a quick look at the photographs.

Slowly she sat down and laid the package on top of
the desk. Then she lifted up the tissue-paper, lightly,
as though afraid of leaving evidence, fingerprints
perhaps.

They were coloured snapshots, and the first one was
of a tall, young, blonde woman, taken at a sandy
beach, with the sea behind her and palm trees towering
overhead against a bright blue sky. It had to be either
one of the Southern California or Florida beaches.

The blonde woman had a hand over her eyes to
shield them from the sun. Her long, straw-coloured
hair hung down to her shoulders, and her face was
lifted in a wide, happy smile. She had on a pair of brief
white shorts and a yellow halter top, revealing long,
slim, shapely legs and a lusciously curved full figure.

Jennie stared at the photograph for several long
seconds, then slowly began to go through the others in
the stack. There were several more of the blonde, in
various poses, some pensive, serious, others more light-
hearted, even comic. She was very beautiful, one of

those self-assured women who never lacked for admirers, the kind of woman Jennie knew she would never be—not in this lifetime, at any rate.

As she turned them over, her spirits plummeted to the point where she was so depressed that she was sorry she'd ever looked at them. It serves me right, she thought bitterly, for prying in the first place. If Alex had wanted her to see the pictures, he would have shown them to her.

She'd come to the last photograph in the stack, anyway, and it turned out to be the last straw, the final stake through her heart. It was of the same blonde and Alex, a much younger Alex, tall and handsome, dressed in a pair of low-slung black trunks, his broad chest and shoulders tanned and gleaming.

They were standing side by side on the same beach, their arms around each other. The blonde was looking directly into the camera, a brilliant smile on her wide mouth, but Alex had eyes only for her. His head was turned in profile, and he was gazing down at her with a look of such intense devotion and desire that it took Jennie's breath away. No man had ever looked at her that way, and with her track record it was a safe bet that no man ever would.

Disgusted with herself for prying in the first place, she was about to gather up the stack of pictures, wrap them in the tissue-paper and put them back in the envelope, when something about that photograph of Alex made her look again. Something wasn't quite right, and it wasn't until she'd examined it carefully for several long moments that she realised what it was.

There was no scar on his chest! Even in a photograph, she could see clearly that his skin was smooth and unmarked. Then that meant that his romance with the blonde had taken place before he had been wounded. She couldn't help herself then. She simply had to take one brief look at the bundle of envelopes— just the outside, she promised herself, not the letters themselves.

She didn't even need to untie the string that held them together. They were all in the same hand, a round, feminine hand, addressed to Alex at an army post office in Saigon, and all with the same name in the upper left-hand corner: Pamela Vance, then an address in Beverly Hills.

'The wages of sin,' Jennie muttered aloud as she carefully put everything back in the wooden box just the way she'd found it. 'It serves me right for meddling where I don't belong.' She replaced the box in the safe, and, deciding not to bother counting the cash in the strongbox, shoved that inside along with it.

Just then she heard a car pull up in the driveway outside. Her heart skipped a beat. It couldn't possibly be Alex! He wasn't due back until Sunday. Maybe he'd decided to come back early.

Quickly she closed the safe door and clicked the lock shut. As she rose to her feet and started towards the door of the office, she heard voices out in the front hallway. Smoothing down the skirt of her dress and putting on a bland expression, she headed in that direction.

When she got there she saw Mrs Anthony standing in the doorway, and on the other side stood Peter Fleming. Although Jennie was relieved to see that it wasn't Alex, after all, she wasn't that thrilled to see Peter, and her step slowed as she approached.

'Hello, Jennie,' he said, peering over Mrs Anthony's shoulder at her.

'Hello, Peter,' she said.

For several seconds, the three of them seemed to stand quite still, as though frozen in a tableau. No one spoke or moved. Then, finally, Mrs Anthony turned away from the door and started walking towards the kitchen, muttering under her breath about work to be done.

Jennie raised her head and gave Peter a cool glance. 'What is it, Peter?'

'May I come in for a minute?' he asked in a subdued voice.

'Why?'

He frowned and gazed down at his feet for a moment, then raised his head and gave her a look of such misery and supplication that she didn't have the heart to send him away. After all, they had been friends since childhood, had once been engaged to be married, and he must have loved her once.

She sighed. 'All right. Come in. But just for a few minutes. I don't really see that we have anything to talk about.'

She led him into the living-room and motioned for him to sit down on the sofa. She placed herself across from him on a straight-backed chair and waited. She wasn't going to help him out. Whatever it was that he had come to say to her, he would have to get through it all by himself.

He stared down at the floor, and, without looking at her, began to speak. 'I haven't had a chance to talk to you since your father's funeral,' he said slowly. 'And there are a few things I need to get off my chest.'

Jennie folded her arms in front of her and gave him a stony look. *His* needs! she thought. Always his needs! Several apt remarks were on her lips, but she bit her tongue and clamped her mouth shut tight, refusing to utter one word.

He looked up at her then. 'I know I behaved badly to you, Jennie. Very badly. And I'm sorry. I just want you to know that. At the time I just felt I had to. . .' He shrugged and raised his hands in a helpless gesture. 'It's hard to explain,' he finished lamely. He took in a lungful of air. 'Anyway, you and I have a long history, and it's been eating at me for months that we haven't even been on speaking terms. I'd like a chance to try to make it up to you, to be friends again.'

Boiling mad by now at his bland assumption that all he had to do was come creeping out here on his knees, make his abject little apology and they could be *friends* again, for heaven's sake, she jumped to her feet and glared down at him.

'All right, Peter,' she bit out. 'You've said your piece, and your apology is accepted, if that's what it means. However, I don't see how we can ever be friends again. What did you have in mind? Inviting me to the wedding? Being godmother to your first child?'

'No,' Peter said in a low voice. He rose to his feet. 'That isn't what I had in mind.'

'Then I don't see that we have anything more to say to each other.' She walked past him towards the door. 'Now, if you don't mind, I have a lot of work to do today.'

He gave her one last look, and started for the door. As he passed her by, he hesitated and opened his mouth again, as though he had more to say. Then, obviously thinking better of it, he continued on and went out, closing the door quietly behind him.

The minute he was gone, the telephone started

ringing. Still angry, she went back into the living-room and snatched it up from the hall table.

'Yes?' she snapped.

'Hey,' came Mark's cheerful voice, 'don't bite my head off.'

Slowly, she sank down on to the couch. From outside she could hear Peter's car start up and drive away. She took a few deep breaths to calm herself.

'Sorry, Mark,' she said at last. 'You caught me at a bad time.'

'Listen, I don't have much time. I'm calling from Portland, and have a meeting in a few minutes. I just wanted to let you know that it looks as though I'll be stuck here for another week and won't be able to make our date Saturday night.'

With all the recent emotional upheaval in her life, she'd completely forgotten that Mark even existed, much less that they'd made a date for Saturday night.

'Oh, that's all right, Mark,' she said distractedly. She forced out a laugh. 'Business before pleasure.'

'I've got to go now,' he said. 'I'll call you when I get back. Probably one day next week.'

When they'd hung up, Jennie leaned her head back on the sofa, closed her eyes, and tried to make some sense out of what was happening to her. She almost had to laugh. First Peter, then Alex, now even Mark didn't want her. She knew she was being childish. All he'd done was break a date that she'd forgotten about in the first place.

Still it rankled. And she was still angry at Peter. What a nerve, to imagine that they could ever be *friends*! It was just like a man. All men were alike. They took what they wanted, when they wanted it, then, when they were ready to move on, simply went, just as though the entire world revolved around *their* needs, *their* wishes, *their* convenience.

She was better off without the whole lot of them. From now on, she would make her own way, and never, ever again rely on one of those monsters for her happiness or fulfilment.

By Friday, Jennie still hadn't left the ranch. Each morning she woke up fully intending to go, and each day she found something else that needed her attention; a business letter that had to be answered, a telephone call she had to make regarding the winery, Mrs Anthony's wages to pay on Thursday.

Now there were only two more days left. Alex would be back on Sunday, and, although it no longer seemed so imperative for her to be gone by then, she knew that if she was going to get on with her life it had to be done.

That morning she dragged out her suitcases from the back of her wardrobe. She had just started packing her clothes inside when the front doorbell rang. Hoping it wasn't one more piece of business she had to attend to before she could leave, she went down the hall to answer it.

When she opened the door and saw the blonde woman standing there, she could only stare at her, open-mouthed. Then she looked again. There was no doubt about it. It was the same woman as the one in the photographs, in the flesh, a little older, to be sure, but with the same wide mouth, the same straw-coloured hair, more fashionably styled, and the same curved, perfect figure.

'Good morning,' the woman said. 'My name is Pamela Vance. I'm looking for Alex Knight.'

Jennie didn't know what to do, but she couldn't leave her standing out there. 'Come in,' she said, opening the door wider.

Pamela Vance flashed her a brilliant smile, and breezed past her, leaving the fragrance of an expensive perfume behind her as she went.

Jennie closed the door and turned round. 'I'm afraid Alex isn't here right now,' she said. 'He had to go out of town on business and won't be back until Sunday.'

'I see.' She eyed Jennie appraisingly. 'Forgive me, I don't mean to pry, but Alex and I are old friends. Would you mind telling me who you are?' She gave a little laugh. 'I don't know quite how to put it. Are you and Alex. . .?' She let the words hang in the air unspoken.

'I only help Alex in the office,' Jennie said stiffly.

Pamela only nodded with satisfaction, then, dismissing Jennie as merely the hired help, walked over to the entrance to the living-room and stood there surveying its contents.

'What a dreary place,' she said at last, turning back to Jennie. 'But then Alex never did have much taste for decorating. It does have possibilities, however.'

At a total loss what in the world to do with the woman now that she was here, Jennie stood there tongue-tied. Pamela Vance was obviously important to Alex, or he wouldn't have kept her letters, those photographs. Surely it was up to her to be hospitable?

'Can I get you something?' she asked finally. 'Coffee? Some iced tea?'

'That would be lovely. Thank you so much.'

Jennie led the way into the kitchen, poured out two glasses of iced tea and set them down on the table.

Pamela had already seated herself and smiled graciously at Jennie, nodding at the chair across from her, as though she were the hostess offering a seat to a guest.

'So tell me,' she said, taking a sip of tea, 'how is Alex?'

'He's fine,' Jennie replied.

'From what I hear, his business is thriving. If you do his office work, you must know that.'

Jennie only nodded, and there was a short silence. Then she said, 'You've known Alex a long time, I take it? I mean, before he came here to Santa Lucia?'

'Oh, yes. For ages. We first met years ago, when we were both still in college.'

A hundred questions about Alex's past leapt into Jennie's mind at her words, but she kept still and waited, watching the lovely blonde as she delicately sipped her tea, so elegant with her expensive black linen dress and simply sculptured coiffure that Jennie felt like a childish clod in her jeans and checked cotton shirt.

Finally, she said, 'You must have been very close.'

Pamela raised a perfect eyebrow and gave Jennie a secret, faraway smile. 'Oh, yes,' she replied. 'You could say that.' She laughed, a light, tinkling, ladylike laugh, then lowered her voice confidentially. 'I behaved very badly towards Alex. In fact, that's really why I came here today.'

She drained the last of her tea, set her glass down and rose gracefully to her feet. 'But then,' she said, 'you don't want to hear about that.' She glanced at her watch. 'I really must be going. Thank you for the tea.'

Jennie got up, and they walked out into the hallway together. Pamela moved ahead of her in a swinging, confident stride, and Jennie, trailing behind, had the peculiar sensation that Pamela was the hostess and she was the guest.

At the front door, Pamela turned to her and gave her another of the dazzling smiles that never quite made it to her eyes. 'Tell Alex I'm sorry I missed him,' she said. She reached in her bag and handed Jennie an engraved card. 'Ask him to call me.' She opened the door and stepped out on to the front porch. 'In any case, I'll be back soon.'

She strode down the path to the small red sports car, and, without a backward glance, got inside and drove away. When the car was out of sight around a bend in the road, Jennie went slowly back inside the house.

She felt as though she'd just learned an important clue to the mystery of Alex's past. How close were they? Had they been married? Pamela said she'd treated him badly. What did that mean? It could mean anything from a minor misunderstanding to adultery. In any case, it wasn't her business. She had her own life to get on with.

By Saturday, Jennie still hadn't left the ranch. Somehow, before Pamela Vance's appearance, it hadn't seemed quite so imperative for her to go. The scene with Alex the night before he'd left had faded with each passing day, until it had almost seemed like a dream. Now, however, with his return imminent, the old urgency began to gnaw at her again.

She simply didn't think that she could face him. Her feelings about him were still in a turmoil, veering crazily from indignation at the way he had rejected her, to gratitude for all his past kindnesses to her. Somewhere inside her, too, was the lingering memory of the passion he had aroused in her, a memory she always quickly stifled whenever it arose.

Although she was certain that his desire for her that night had been genuine, in spite of the way he had reacted afterwards, he obviously wasn't for her. And now, with the lovely Pamela back in the picture, he would have other things on his mind.

In any case, after what had happened she couldn't stay out here alone with him any longer, so that evening after supper she finally did go to her room and finish packing her belongings. When she was through, she lugged the suitcases and boxes down to the front hall and set them beside the door.

She was all ready to leave. All she had to do now was call Peggy and make sure she could stay with her for a few days.

She had just gone into the kitchen, picked up the telephone and started to dial, when she heard a car door slam outside, then the front door open and close. For a moment her mind went blank. It had to be Alex! But he wasn't supposed to come home until tomorrow.

She slammed down the receiver, and, with a thudding heart, walked slowly out of the kitchen into the hall.

CHAPTER EIGHT

ALEX WAS standing there, tall and rumpled in his dark suit, his tie askew, staring down at her bags, a bewildered expression on his face. He looks so tired, she thought. He must have been travelling all day. Willing her pounding heart to settle down, she took a step towards him.

'Hello, Alex,' she said quietly. 'I wasn't expecting you until tomorrow.'

He pointed accusingly at her bags. 'What's this all about?'

'I'm leaving.'

'Just like that?' he growled. He moved swiftly to cover the distance between them until he came to stand directly before her, looking down at her, his grey eyes boring into her. 'Why?' he ground out. 'Why are you leaving?'

She bit her lip and looked away, tongue-tied. Now that he was actually here and she was face to face with him, the impact of his sheer physical presence threatened to overwhelm her. She could sense him waiting for her answer. She had to say something.

Still unable to face him, she muttered, 'I don't know. I just decided it would probably be for the best. I have to get on with my life, and you have to get on with yours.'

'Listen,' he said in a softer tone, 'if it's about what happened between us the night before I left, I can explain. I've had a lot of time to think about it while

I've been away, and have decided there's no point in lying or hiding my feelings any longer, either to you or to myself.'

At his unexpected words, she raised her head and gave him a wondering look. When she saw the expression on his face of humble, almost tormented supplication, her heart went out to him, and she knew then that she didn't really want to leave.

He *was* a very attractive man, and he seemed extremely anxious now to straighten things out between them. Maybe she had reacted too hastily to what had seemed to her like one more rejection. Perhaps he'd only pushed her away that night out of concern that his sudden explosive display of passion might frighten her. Or himself!

Then she remembered Pamela, and her heart sank.

'Pamela Vance was here last week,' she said at last, her voice dull and flat.

If she had struck him he couldn't have looked more shocked. His head jerked back, his eyes widened, and he took a step back from her. Then, almost immediately, his face closed down and the grey eyes blazed with anger.

'Pamela? What the hell was she doing here?' he barked.

'She was looking for you, of course.'

She reached down, picked up the card lying on the hall table and handed it to him. He took it from her and stared at it, holding it by one corner, as though afraid it would go up in flames at any moment. He gave her one long look, then dropped the card back on the table.

'That's ancient history,' he said flatly. He raised a hand and rubbed it wearily over his unshaven jaw, frowning down at the floor for several moments. 'Listen,' he said, facing her again. 'We've got to talk. Right now I'm dead beat. And starved. I need to change my clothes and get something to eat. Will you just give me half an hour to get out of these clothes and shower? And promise not to leave until I come back?'

Jennie gave him a dubious look. If she didn't go now, as she had planned, she was afraid that her nerve would fail her. While she hesitated, he put a hand lightly, tentatively, on her arm.

'Please, Jennie,' he said. 'Promise you'll stay.'

Finally she nodded. 'All right,' she said in a small voice. Then she lifted her chin. 'But I still think it would be better if I left tonight.'

He nodded. 'We'll see. If you still want to go after we've talked, I won't stop you.' He smiled bleakly. 'In fact, I'll help you move.'

He picked up his bag then, and strode off down the hall away from her, his broad shoulders back, his step firm and brisk. She stood there at the door, watching him until he disappeared around the corner of the hallway. Then she gave her pile of baggage one last, rueful glance and went into the kitchen to put the casserole she had prepared for his supper tomorrow in the oven.

While she worked, she hardly dared think about what his words meant. What had he been thinking over while he was in New York? What were the lies he'd told her, the feelings he'd been hiding? She went over and over their whole relationship, right back to the time he'd first come to Santa Lucia.

She'd only been sixteen years old then, still in school, and even then so solidly bound to Peter that no one else even existed for her. Alex had been a grown man, almost thirty. When he and her father became friends, she'd simply put Alex in that generation, habitually thinking of him as a contemporary of her father's. Yet there had been more difference in the ages of the two men than there was between her and Alex.

Then there was the night of the *fiesta*, right after Peter had broken off their engagement, and one or two other occasions, when he'd looked at her in a certain way, shown small signs of having more than a paternal or brotherly interest in her, signs she'd ignored for the most part. That was, until last Saturday night.

That *had* been genuine desire! She hadn't been mistaken about that. But what did it mean? And how did she feel about it? She liked Alex, had always admired and respected him. And, she had to admit, her own passion had been awakened that night a week ago—awakened, in fact, to an intensity which she'd never experienced with any other man, certainly not with Peter or Mark.

But what about Pamela Vance? A cold chill gripped her heart every time she envisaged that lovely, sophisticated blonde in her mind, so full of confidence. She had spoken of Alex with such possessive intimacy. How could Jennie hope to compete with a woman like that?

The casserole would be done soon, and she started putting a salad together, washing greens, slicing tomatoes. With each small task, with each passing moment, her pulse-rate escalated a little higher. Soon she would learn just what it was that he had on his mind, and she looked forward to it with a mingled sense of excited anticipation and apprehension.

She was just taking the dish out of the oven when

she heard his bedroom door close and his footsteps coming down the stairs. He was going into the living-room, probably to make himself a drink. She dished out his supper with shaking fingers, dropping the serving spoon in the process. Then, when she was finished, she took a deep breath and picked up the tray.

In the living-room, he was kneeling before the fireplace, a drink in one hand, and poking at the kindling he had just lit with the other. When she appeared, he rose to his feet and turned round to face her, holding up his glass.

'Would you like a drink?'

She set the tray down on the coffee-table. 'I'll get it. You'd better eat this while it's hot.'

While Jennie went over to the drinks cupboard to pour herself a glass of sherry, he threw a log on the fire, watched for a moment to make sure it caught, then sat down, picked up a fork and started on his meal.

Feeling awkward and tongue-tied, now that they were actually together in the same room, and still nervous about what was coming, Jennie took a hasty sip of sherry, then went over to stand in front of the fire.

Alex gazed up at her for a moment, then pushed the tray away and nodded at his half-empty plate. 'That was wonderful,' he said, 'but I've got other things on my mind at the moment.' He held out a hand to her. 'Come and sit beside me.'

Slowly she walked over to him and sat down on the edge of the cushion. She glanced over at him. He was staring into the fire, his grey eyes brooding, a frown on his lean face. He had shaved hurriedly, and there was a small cut on his jaw, just below his ear. He needed a haircut, too, and the hair growing low on the back of his neck was still damp from his shower.

Yet, watching him, Jennie felt the warm stirrings of desire rising up within her. What was it about this man that affected her so? she wondered. She took another quick gulp of her sherry and waited.

Finally he turned to her. 'I think I'd better start out with a little history.' He smiled crookedly. 'I've pushed the past out of my mind for so long that I think it's been blown out of all proportion, just lain there festering. It's time—way past time—to get it out in the open.'

He took a long swallow of his drink, then went on. 'First, I guess, is the matter of Pamela. There's no other way to put it except to say that I was crazy in love with her when I was a boy. We met in college. She came from a wealthy family, I came straight from an orphanage in Los Angeles. She was beautiful and polished even then, I was a rough type who only made it to college on an athletic scholarship.'

He set his glass down on the tray and turned to her. 'Anyway, as it turned out, I soon learned that star football players were considered desirable trophies for the sorority girls, and so Pamela and I became engaged. Her father was chairman of the board of a large brokerage firm. I was going to work for him as soon as I graduated. And then——' He broke off and his face darkened.

'Then?' Jennie prompted after a moment.

'Then I was drafted, went overseas, got wounded— you've seen the scar—and when I came back I was a wreck, mentally and physically. It took me years in a veterans' hospital to get my mind and body patched up.'

'And what happened to Pamela?' Jennie asked softly.

Alex shrugged. 'Oh, she visited me for a month or two. But she could never quite hide the horrified look in her eyes whenever she looked at me. Eventually she just stopped coming, and the next thing I heard she was married to someone else.'

'Alex,' Jennie murmured, 'I'm so sorry.'

'It was a long time ago, but it left its scars.' He took her hand and pressed it tightly in his. 'So now you understand what I meant when I told you some time ago that I was jilted, too. Don't get me wrong, though. I'm not blaming Pamela. She was young, and a little spoiled. She couldn't tolerate my physical *and* mental wounds. And, although eventually I recovered in both areas, the whole experience rather soured me on romance.' He gazed into her eyes. 'That is, until you came along.'

Jennie's eyes widened. 'Me?'

He nodded. 'I think I've always loved you, Jennie, from the time I first saw you as a teenager in school.'

She stared at him. 'Alex, I had no idea. You never said anything. I couldn't possibly have known.'

'Of course not. I didn't either, actually. I didn't think of you at all in those terms. You were only a child.' He reached out and put a hand on her cheek. 'Such a serious girl, even then, a real person. There wasn't an ounce of vanity in you.'

'But you don't think of me as a child any more,' she said.

'Obviously not,' he replied with a grin. 'When you became engaged to Fleming, I remember thinking that he wasn't good enough for you, and when he left you I was secretly relieved. Even then, though, I didn't dare admit how I really felt. Even aside from the difference in our ages, it never occurred to me that you would ever think of me in any way except as an older brother, at best. So I hid my feelings and didn't press you. But last Saturday night, when you showed up in the kitchen in that nightgown, I just lost control. I'm sorry about that, Jennie. It won't happen again.'

That wasn't exactly what she wanted to hear. There were a million questions she wanted to ask him, but she didn't know where to begin. If he felt that way about her, why did he push her away? Didn't he realise that it only made her feel rejected once again?

She searched his face, but could see no trace of the naked desire that had blazed out of his eyes that night a week ago. Instead, he was gazing at her soberly, obviously waiting for her to say something.

'There's no need to apologise,' she said at last. 'I was as much to blame as you were.'

She wondered wildly why they were talking about blame. No crime had been committed. They were a man and a woman, both adults, both free, who desired each other. What could be more natural? There had to be something else, and she thought she knew what it might be.

'Do you still love her?' she blurted out.

He raised his eyebrows. 'Pamela?' he exclaimed. 'No. Of course not. I already told you. That's ancient history.' His forehead creased in a frown. 'It beats me why she showed up here at all. We haven't communicated for years. But then,' he added grimly, 'Pamela always was unpredictable.'

Somehow, the way he said that made it sound like a

virtue he admired, albeit reluctantly. Totally predictable herself, Jennie felt a swift pang of envy.

'I see,' she said tightly.

Alex gave her a close look. 'Listen, Jennie, I have no feelings whatsoever for Pamela Vance.' He put a hand under her chin and tilted her head back so that she had to meet his penetrating gaze. 'Do you believe me?'

'Of course,' she said with a smile.

Inwardly she wasn't so sure. Although she knew that Alex would never lie to her about something like that, after what had happened so recently with Peter her confidence was at its lowest ebb.

'And you'll stay?' he said.

'All right,' she replied. There was no reason not to, now.

He leaned towards her then, and reached out for her. For one second she stiffened, resisting, but as his arms came around her she relaxed against him. He kissed her tenderly, his lips warm and gentle on her mouth. Then he raised his head and looked down at her, his lean face sober.

'I do love you, Jennie,' he said softly. 'I want to marry you, to take care of you forever.'

'Marry me?'

Jennie gazed uncertainly at him. She wasn't at all sure how she felt about that! She loved Alex, had always loved him in a way. She felt safe here in his arms, protected, cherished. But marriage? Marriage meant an intimacy she wasn't sure that she was ready for.

He gave her a reassuring smile and his large hands began to stroke up and down her arms. As the rough, callused palms rasped against her bare skin, a flame began to ignite deep inside her, and she *knew*! Of course she wanted him, in every way. She'd known that a week ago.

She was just about to tell him so when he tucked her head under his chin and started smoothing back her hair from her forehead. 'You don't need to decide right away,' he said. 'Think it over. Take your time. We can talk about it later, whenever you're ready.'

He put his hands on her shoulders and bent his head to kiss her again, lightly. Then he rose to his feet, pulling her along with him.

'Now, let's get those bags of yours back in your room. It's getting late, and I've got a touch of jet lag to sleep off.'

An hour later, Jennie was in her bedroom slowly unpacking her belongings and putting them away. After carrying her suitcases from the hall and depositing them just inside the door, Alex had given her one last quick peck on the mouth and gone off to bed.

As she hung her dresses in the wardrobe and put underwear away in the chest of drawers, she thought about Alex's explanation of his past life—the longest speech she'd ever heard him make—and his offer to marry her.

Did she want to marry Alex? It would mean safety and security for the rest of her life, and, as Peggy had once said, he was the prime catch in the whole valley. It was tempting, and she should probably feel flattered, but instead she was oddly disappointed, even let down.

Where was the passion, the fire? He might as well have patted her on the head and told her to be a good girl. What more did she want? He'd said he loved her. Wasn't that enough? But he'd been, in his very own words, 'crazy in love' with Pamela Vance. There was a difference there, but she couldn't quite put her finger on it.

He'd been tired, though, travelling all day after a week of being away from home involved in business negotiations. And, as he'd said himself, there was no need to make a decision tonight. She would wait and see what happened.

What happened in the next few days was exactly nothing. They went on almost exactly as they had before, pleasant and polite, but with a distance between them. After his intensely personal revelations to her about his past, he seemed to withdraw back into his shell, the old barriers he had erected against the world firmly back in place.

The only indication he gave her that anything had changed in their relationship was an occasional questioning glance, as though he was waiting for her to make up her mind where they were going. He didn't touch her or make any direct allusion to his proposal of marriage.

As the days passed, Jennie found to her dismay that this distance he placed between them only intensified her desire for him, made her long even more for a trace of the passion she had glimpsed in the past. Finally she had to face the fact that if she expected to be swept off her feet by this silent, enigmatic man, she was doomed to disappointment. It just wasn't going to happen, not unless she engineered it herself.

On Wednesday evening after his return from New York, she made up her mind. She set the stage carefully. The weather had turned cold and blustery, a heavy rain spattering against the windows, a brisk

March wind whistling through the cracks in the windows. It was a good night to be indoors.

She had steaks marinating on the kitchen counter, a fire laid in the living-room, martinis cooling in the fridge, and while Alex was cleaning up she had made up carefully and brushed her hair until it shone. She decided to wear her green silk dress, the most seductive one she owned, with its low, square neck and cinched waist.

When she heard his step in the hall, she took out the martini pitcher and carried it into the living-room. Then she lit the fire and called to him, 'In here, Alex.'

She stood in front of the fire waiting for him, and when he appeared in the doorway, fresh from his shower, he stopped short and stared at her for several long moments. Then he slowly came towards her, a crooked smile hovering about his lips.

'I've made martinis,' she said, pointing to the tray on the coffee-table. 'I hope you like them.'

He only nodded briefly. She went over to the table and poured out the drinks with shaking fingers, spilling several drops in the process, then carried them back to where he stood.

He took his glass from her, and raised it in the air. 'What's the occasion?'

She took a quick swallow of the burning liquor and lifted her chin. 'I've decided I'd like to marry you, Alex,' she said.

At first his face went blank. Then his eyes lit up and he gave her a warm, pleased smile.

'I'm glad, Jennie.'

They stood there motionless for several long moments, their eyes locked together, and as she watched the flickering firelight play over his fine features, the strength and depth of his character shining out of his eyes, all her doubts fled. She knew that she had done the right thing.

She loved him! It was as simple as that. What was more, she desired him! She wanted all of him, not only the safety and protection and warm steady love he could give her, but him as a man, an intensely attractive man.

In those few seconds she stared at him as though seeing him for the first time, examining him carefully, feature by feature. The crisp black hair combed neatly back from his broad forehead, the long straight nose, the fine grey eyes with their heavy black brows, the thin, wide, sensitive mouth.

He was dressed as he usually was in the evening, in a clean white shirt, the collar open at the throat, the cuffs rolled up to reveal strong forearms, which were tanned and covered with fine, silky black hairs. There was nothing out of the ordinary, but tonight the impact of his very presence was so overpowering that she was speechless, lost in admiration of his absolute maleness.

Then he reached for her glass, took it out of her hand and set it down on the mantelpiece along with his own. He held out his arms to her, and as she fell against him she raised her arms up around his neck and lifted her face for his kiss.

His hands held her tightly around the waist so that their bodies weren't quite touching, and when she tried to move closer, to feel the long, hard length of his body against hers, his grip tightened, almost as though he were keeping her from him.

He put the palm of one hand on her cheek and held her eyes in his, then bent down to place his mouth on hers in a brief, almost chaste kiss. Immediately he dropped his hands and reached for their drinks, which were still sitting on the mantelpiece.

'We really do have something to celebrate,' he said, taking a long swallow. 'And there are a lot of things we have to decide.'

Jennie stared at him in frustration, totally taken aback by the distance he had put between them. She had practically offered herself to him on a plate. Why hadn't he responded? Did he intend to marry her or adopt her, for heaven's sake?

'Jennie?' he said, giving her a puzzled frown. 'Is something wrong?'

What could she say? She searched his face, as though hoping to find her answer there, and what she saw in the deep grey eyes was unmistakable. He did love her. There was no doubt about it. The warmth he felt for her radiated from every pore. But it wasn't the passion she had hoped to find. She would have to be patient. Surely it would come in time?

'No,' she said at last, with a quick, reassuring smile. 'Of course nothing's wrong.' She forced out a laugh. 'I guess it's all still just a little strange to me.'

He put an arm around her and kissed the top of her head. 'You'll get used to it in time. I have to admit that it's somewhat unsettling to me, too. But I think it's right, for both of us.' He turned her around to face him then, and placed his hands lightly on her shoulders. 'I do care deeply for you, Jennie, and I'll do everything in my power to make you happy.'

'I know that, Alex,' she said softly.

Every nerve in her body ached to be crushed up against that broad chest, to feel that wide mouth come down on hers with the passion and the hunger she knew was in him. It was on her lips to tell him so, but he turned from her then, took her by the hand and led her over to the couch.

'We'll have to make some plans,' he said. 'I don't see any point in delaying a wedding date, so we might as well get it done as soon as possible.'

Fighting down her disappointment at his distant, almost businesslike tone, she told herself that he was only being considerate of her. Part of him still thought of her as a child, in spite of his protestations to the contrary. Surely it would be different after they were married? She would be his wife then, and all that would change. Wouldn't it?

CHAPTER NINE

THEY decided on March the twenty-first, the first day
of spring, as their wedding date. It was less than three
weeks off, and there suddenly seemed to be an endless
number of things that had to be done in a very short
time.

The first of these tasks was the one Jennie dreaded
the most. She had to tell Peggy. Mrs Anthony had
been ecstatic when Alex had made the announcement
to her on her first 'day' after his proposal. If Peggy's
reaction came anywhere near that outpouring of good
wishes and genuine joy at the news, it would be a
miracle. Jennie couldn't forget that Peggy had had her
eye on Alex herself.

That Thursday morning Jennie called her friend at
work and made a date for lunch. She wanted to drive
into town, anyway, to look for a wedding dress. It was
to be a small affair, with only a few close friends, Mrs
Anthony, of course, the men who worked for Alex
and, she hoped, Peggy as her bridesmaid.

They arranged to meet at the small restaurant near
the shop where Peggy worked as buyer. Jennie arrived
a few minutes early and sat in a back booth composing
her speech. Should she refer to Peggy's interest in
Alex? Better not. It had never really amounted to
anything.

Before she was able to settle on exactly the right way
to present her news, Peggy came walking towards her,

the first occasion in living memory that she had ever been on time for an appointment.

'What's up?' she said, sliding into the booth across from Jennie. 'You sounded so serious on the telephone this morning.'

There was no delicate way to do it. As soon as Peggy had shed her coat and settled herself comfortably, Jennie put on a bright, cheerful smile and leaned across the table towards her.

'I'm going to marry Alex,' she said in a breathless rush.

For a moment Peggy only stared at her. Then her mouth fell open, as though she wanted to say something but couldn't quite get the words out. Finally, she slumped back and glared at Jennie.

'I don't believe it,' she stated flatly. 'Are we talking about the same person? Alex Knight? How could you do this to me?'

It was exactly what Jennie had been afraid of. 'Peggy,' she said helplessly, 'I don't know what to say. If I thought for a minute you were really serious about him, I never would have——'

'Oh, never mind,' Peggy broke in with an impatient wave of her hand. 'I'm only kidding, I guess. Don't forget, I was the one who told you after that lovely dinner you ruined that he only had eyes for you.' She shook her head. 'But marriage? Isn't that a little drastic?'

'What did you have in mind?' Jennie enquired with a wry smile. 'A discreet affair?'

'Well, no. I guess that's not your style, is it?' She reached in her handbag and took out a packet of cigarettes, lit one and gave Jennie a long, appreciative glance. 'Well,' she said, blowing out smoke, 'aren't you the deep one, though? Marrying Alex Knight! You're going to be the envy of every unattached woman under forty in the whole valley.'

'I don't know about that, Peggy. I just know that it seems like the right thing to do.'

Peggy frowned at her. 'That doesn't sound very romantic. Do you love him?'

'Yes. Of course I love him. He's been wonderful to me.'

'Sounds thrilling!' Peggy commented tartly. 'If I were engaged to marry that man, I'd manage to work up a little more enthusiasm than that.' She narrowed her eyes. 'Don't tell me you're still carrying a torch for that rat, Peter Fleming?'

Jennie shook her head vigorously. 'No. Not any more.' She gave a little laugh. 'As a matter of fact, Peter came out to see me.'

'Why on earth did he do that?'

Jennie lifted her shoulders. 'Who knows? Guilty conscience, probably. Anyway, it turned out all right. A little cool, but at least we ended up on speaking terms. That's all in the past now, and can finally be laid to rest.'

The waitress came to take their order just then. They both decided on club sandwiches with a green salad, and Peggy insisted on ordering a carafe of wine to celebrate. When it arrived, she raised her glass in a toast.

'Well, here's to you, Jennie. I'm glad it's all working out so well for you. You deserve it after the bad breaks you've had in the past year.' They both took a swallow of wine, then Peggy said, 'Tell me, when is it to be?'

'Two weeks from Sunday,' Jennie replied. 'It'll be a

very small private affair, but I'm counting on you to be there to hold my hand in case I get last-minute jitters.'

'Have you picked out your dress yet?'

'No. I'm going to do that this afternoon.'

'Come back with me to the store after lunch, then,' Peggy said. 'I have just the thing for you.'

During the days that followed, Alex remained pretty much the same as always; polite, friendly, a little remote. Although Jennie was aware of a new warmth in the deep grey eyes whenever he looked at her, and his goodnight kisses were affectionate, that was as far as his lovemaking went.

She would have given anything to see that brilliant flash of passion in his eyes just once before she committed herself to him for life, but as the wedding date approached and he still kept his distance she began to have serious doubts that she ever would.

Did he really love her? As a woman? Or in his heart was he still in love with Pamela? She was obviously the one great love of his life. Possibly he never would really get over her, and Jennie would always be second-best to him, a kind of consolation prize. She kept telling herself that she had to accept him the way he was, and hope that after they were married he would change.

One morning, a week after her lunch date with Peggy, Jennie received a telephone call from Mr Simms, the estate agent who had sold her house. Once the papers had been signed, she hadn't even driven by the old house, with all its painful memories, and she was surprised to hear from him now.

'Jennie,' he said, 'I'm afraid I have some bad news for you.'

'What is it?'

'You know the Dabneys, the people who bought your house? If you recall, you agreed to let them live in the house for six months only paying the taxes and utilities, until they received the money for the down payment from the sale of their own home. Well, they've up and left.'

'What do you mean?'

'I mean they're gone. Just took off. Left the house in a fine mess, to boot. Now, if you remember, I tried to warn you when you signed the agreement that you were taking a big chance on them.'

Jennie did remember. She'd been so dazed by the death of her father, following so soon after losing Peter, that she would have agreed to anything, just so she wouldn't have to think about it any longer. Now, with her wedding less than two weeks away, the last thing she needed was to have to bother about getting the house ready to sell again, but it looked as though it had to be done.

'Yes, Mr Simms,' she said with a sigh. 'It's not your fault. I take full responsibility. What do you think I should do about it?'

'Well, I can put it on the market again, but it's going to need a good cleaning first.'

'All right. I'll drive into town today and take a look at it,' she said. 'Then I'll let you know.'

After she hung up, she decided she might as well go right away, see the worst and deal with it as best she could. Alex was busy out in the vineyard today. There was no point in bothering him. She glanced down at her ragged blue denims and thin cotton shirt. She wouldn't even need to change. She would just go and inspect the house and come right back.

She got her handbag from her bedroom and went directly out to the car. It was another warm day, and as she drove past the vineyard she saw Alex out in the front field, so tall that he towered over the other men working with him. She gave a light toot on the horn, and he turned to wave at her as she went by.

When she got to the house, she soon saw that it was in an even worse mess than Mr Simms had claimed. The Dabneys had obviously not been very particular housekeepers. Every room in the house needed a good cleaning, especially the kitchen, where the rubbish was overflowing under the counter, the floor sticky with spilled food and dirty dishes piled in the sink.

There was a broken lamp in the living-room and a heavy layer of dust had settled on every piece of furniture. Upstairs none of the beds were made, and as Jennie surveyed the depressing scene she was grateful that at least they had left the bedding. Nothing actually appeared to have been stolen.

After the first shock had passed, Jennie realised that it wasn't the disaster that it had at first appeared to be. Granted, she had lost any possible profit on the house, and the Dabneys had lived in it rent-free for six months, but still, with professional help, it would only take a few days to get it cleaned up.

The telephone was still in working order, and before leaving she called Mr Simms to tell him what she had decided to do. He gave her the name of a good cleaning service, and agreed to put the house back on the market as soon as it was ready.

She drove back with a lighter heart than she had set out with. The sun was shining, and in just a week from Sunday she would marry Alex. She was actually feeling quite pleased with herself at the way she had handled the house problem with such dispatch, and it had done her good to see her old home one more time.

When she arrived back at the ranch there was a small red sports car parked in the driveway alongside Alex's station-wagon. Jennie recognised it immediately as the one Pamela Vance had driven.

She got out of the car and started walking slowly towards the house. As she neared the front steps, she hesitated. Through the open doorway came the sound of voices. She stopped short, unable to decide whether to go inside and barge in on what seemed to be a highly personal conversation, or wait out here until the beautiful blonde left.

As she debated, listening with half an ear, the voices began to rise steadily, obviously in the heat of anger.

'You've got a hell of a nerve,' Alex was shouting, 'coming here after all these years and telling me you made a mistake! Hell, Pamela, have you forgotten how hard I fought to convince you of that very thing ten years ago?' The anguish and bitterness in his voice were unmistakable, and Jennie could only stand there, rooted to the spot, unable to move a muscle.

'That's what I'm trying to tell you!' Pamela cried. 'You were right. I was wrong. The marriage with Derek was a stupid mistake, but what else could I do? I was only a girl, Alex! Immature, I grant you, spoilt, and totally unable to face being married to an invalid. Your injuries frightened me. How was I to know you would make such a total recovery?'

'And what has changed?' Alex demanded in a cold, clipped tone, the words resounding like gunshots in the stillness of the afternoon.

'*I've* changed!' Pamela wailed. 'How can I convince you of that?'

'Well, it's too late!' he retorted. Then, in a low voice that throbbed with emotion, he added, 'Ten years too late, to be exact. I'm going to marry someone else.'

'Who?' she demanded.

'Jennifer Corbett,' he replied stiffly. 'Not that it's any of your concern.'

'That drab little secretary?' she cried. 'That child? No! I don't believe you.'

'Don't say another word!' he shouted. 'Not one more damned word, or I'll——'

'Alex, stop!' Pamela protested in a shaky voice. 'You're hurting me!'

There was a long, tense silence after that, but by then Jennie had heard enough. Finding her legs at last, she turned and stumbled back to her car. She jumped inside, started the engine and headed towards the highway.

She drove aimlessly around the back country roads for what seemed like hours, fighting back the hot tears of humiliation and rage. How dared that woman criticise her? 'Drab little secretary,' she muttered under her breath. 'Only a child!' And who was she to come back here now and upset all their plans?

After a while, her fury finally spent itself, but only to be replaced by something far worse. A dull, lethargic depression seemed to fill her whole being; there was a heaviness on her heart, a deep sense of impending doom that twisted her insides into a knot of anxiety.

When she was finally able to put a name to it, she realised that what she was feeling now was sheer, uncontrollable jealousy. It never occurred to her for a moment that Alex would throw her over for the lovely

Pamela. That wasn't the problem at all. Alex was a man of his word. He would never go back on it once he'd committed himself.

No, what ate at her very soul was not concern that Alex might jilt her too, the way Peter had, but the passion she'd heard in his voice when he'd shouted at Pamela, a passion that had amounted to blind, unreasoning hatred, an intensity of emotion that he'd never revealed to Jennie in their own tepid relationship.

And even though every word she'd heard him utter only confirmed to her his determination to send Pamela away, she simply couldn't help envying the woman her ability to touch the deep chord in Alex that he kept so carefully hidden from her.

And what did they say about the other side of the coin? That the real opposite of love was not hatred, but indifference.

It was late afternoon when she finally returned. She'd been gone since before noon and hadn't had a bite to eat since breakfast. The one thought on her mind was to have this whole thing out with Alex immediately, while the memory of the scene with Pamela was still fresh in her mind and before she lost her nerve.

The red car was gone, thank heaven, and inside the house she could hear the shower running in Alex's bathroom. When it was turned off, she gave him five minutes to get dried and dressed, then marched down the hall to his room.

She stood there for a second, then took a deep breath and rapped smartly on the door. 'Alex,' she called, 'I'd like to talk to you.'

'Come on in,' he called back. 'I'm decent.'

She opened the door and stepped inside. Alex was

just coming out of the adjoining bathroom, rubbing his damp head with a towel. He was wearing a pair of dark trousers, and that was all. His bare chest still glistened with drops of water from his shower, and he was barefoot.

When he saw the look on her face, he stopped short and stared. 'What is it, Jennie? You look upset.'

As she stared at him, at the tall muscled form, the scar that slashed across his bare chest, the sheer animal magnetism of the man, she couldn't seem to get the right words out.

'You've been gone a long time,' he went on. 'When I saw you drive off in such a hurry this morning I wondered if something could be wrong. Then when you didn't come home I started to worry. In fact, I was just about ready to go looking for you.'

'I did come home,' she said curtly. He raised questioning eyebrows, but before he could say anything she ploughed doggedly ahead. 'I had some business with the house to take care of in town, but I was back here by two o'clock.'

The puzzled expression on his face faded as the light slowly dawned and the full implications of her statement sank in. Then he threw the towel down on a chair and went over to the dresser, where he picked up one of his rare cigarettes and lit it, blowing smoke out thoughtfully.

After a few quick drags, he stubbed it out in an ashtray and turned round to face her.

'Then you must have seen that I had a visitor,' he said slowly.

'Yes. I saw her car. I also overheard a good deal of the conversation.'

'And?'

'What do you mean by that?' she challenged.

'Why are you so angry, Jennie?' he asked softly.

He started to walk towards her, one hand out-stretched, but she moved back a step and set her jaw defiantly. He stopped just inches away from her and frowned.

'If you heard what was said, then you know that I made it very clear to Pamela that I wasn't interested in patching up our old differences, much less renewing our relationship, on any terms whatsoever.'

'Yes. I heard that. I agree. You made it very clear.'

He ran a hand over the back of his neck and the frown deepened. 'Then I fail to see what it is that has you so upset,' he said at last. Although his tone was still patient and calm, there was a barely recognisable note in it of his own rising irritation.

'I told you I heard what you *said* to Pamela. What bothers me is what you didn't say, what you obviously felt.'

He folded his arms across his chest and narrowed his eyes at her. 'Don't tell me how I feel, Jennie. What I said was what I meant. If you choose to put your own interpretation on it, I guess that's your privilege, but you might at least tell me what that might be before jumping to any conclusions.'

'All right!' she cried. 'I will.' She took a deep breath, so worked up by now that she didn't care what she said, and forged ahead with reckless abandon. 'You're still in love with her, aren't you?'

'I'm not even going to dignify that with an answer,' he bit out contemptuously. 'You're out of your mind if you think that.'

His calm composure only fuelled her anger. 'Oh, really?' she cried. 'Well, I think you are in love with her, but just don't want to admit it. I *heard* you, Alex. The words themselves didn't mean a thing, but your tone spoke volumes. You've never, ever spoken to me with such feeling, such passion.'

'Damn it!' he shouted. 'I was *mad*! Can't you understand that? What is it you want, Jennie? Are you saying that because I don't throw you out of the house, that means I don't love you? Is that it?'

'In a sense, yes!' She spread her arms wide. 'You say you love me, but there's no difference in the way you treat me from the way my father used to. I'm still a little girl to you, and I always will be. You just can't grasp the fact that I'm a grown woman and start treating me like one. And you never will!'

His face had turned ashen by now. He held his arms rigidly at his sides, his hands clenched into fists. She could see the little pulse throbbing along his hard, set jaw, hear his laboured breathing, palpably *feel* the waves of barely contained fury emanating from him.

Then he smiled, a cold, mocking smile. 'You want to be treated like a woman, Jennie?' he asked softly. 'All right. But remember, you asked for it.'

He took one menacing step towards her. At the sight of the hard, determined look on his face, Jennie's heart started pounding wildly. She'd never seen Alex quite so angry before, and the sight was not a reassuring one. She backed away from him, all primed to turn and run, but before she could move he reached out a hand, grasped the openings of her blouse and ripped them apart.

'Alex!' she cried, cowering away from him. He was like a madman, and she was becoming seriously frightened now.

He didn't utter a word. In the next second the filmy

bra had been torn away along with the blouse, and they lay in a crumpled heap on the floor at her feet. He stood before her staring at her bare breasts, his hands on his hips, his legs apart, his mouth twisted in a cold, contemptuous leer.

'Well,' he said, raising his eyes to hers. 'So you are a woman, after all.'

He reached out for her again. Trying to cover her nakedness with her hands, she turned quickly, in a panic now to get out of there. But he was too quick for her. Before she was able to take the first step, he had grabbed her from behind and pulled her back so roughly that she lost her footing.

She squeezed her eyes shut tight as he pressed her against his hard body. The heavy pounding of his heartbeats thudded against her back, his unshaven face scraped against her cheek, and his hot breath rasped in her ear. Before she could get her wind back, he had brought his hands swiftly around and swept them over her small firm breasts, then down under the waistband of her jeans.

'Is that what you want, Jennie?' he snarled in her ear.

'No!' she cried out in desperation. 'No! Please, Alex! Please, stop!'

'Not until I've proved to you that I damn well do think of you as a woman—and have given you a lesson in just what that means.'

He twisted her around and started to shove her bodily over to the bed, his long legs inexorably propelling her backwards. With the weight of his own body he forced her down on top of the bed. Then, propping himself up on one elbow, he gripped her hands and pinned them down over her head.

He hovered over her, staring stonily down at her for a few seconds, then abruptly lowered himself on top of her. His open mouth came down on hers in a punishing kiss, his tongue pushing past her lips, his teeth grinding against hers. His hands were everywhere now, probing, exploring every inch of her body, his hot mouth following.

Jennie writhed beneath him, frantic to escape the furious assault, knowing that she was no match for his superior physical strength, and literally weeping with frustration. Yet, even at the very height of her helpless fear and anger, her traitorous body responded to his rough, demanding caresses as though it had a will of its own.

She was entirely naked by now. Exhausted from the struggle, she lay limp beneath him, waiting stoically for the inevitable. His mouth was at her breast, pulling at the tip, sending shock-waves of arousal through her, and she knew that she was lost, that she had no power to control either Alex's actions or her own desire.

Then, suddenly, he went quite still. The weight of his body lifted from hers and the bedsprings creaked as he rose to his feet. Wondering helplessly what was coming next, Jennie opened her eyes.

His back was turned towrds her, his heaving shoulders slumped over, every muscle taut, as though he was struggling for control. Then, without a word, he reached into the wardrobe, grabbed a shirt and stalked out of the door, slamming it hard behind him.

When he had gone, she lay there for several moments, totally bewildered, listening to the front door bang, his car start up and drive away, then total silence.

Still in a daze, she cautiously raised herself up. Every muscle, every inch of skin, felt bruised and sore. Her teeth were chattering, and she felt as though she had just been in some kind of terrible accident. Finally, she dragged herself off the bed, picked her torn clothing up off the floor and went slowly down the hall to her own room. She knew what she had to do, and she had to do it quickly, before he came back.

She threw on clean clothes, hurriedly tossed the few personal belongings she would need into an overnight bag, and ran a comb through her tangled hair. She still hadn't entirely unpacked, and there was one full suitcase still sitting inside her wardrobe.

When she was ready she slung her handbag over her shoulder, picked up the overnight bag in one hand, the suitcase in the other, and bumped her way awkwardly out into the hall. At the door, she turned to take one last look at the bedroom she had occupied for the past few months.

There was no point in leaving a note. After his brutal attack, Alex certainly wouldn't expect any communication from her, much less that she could ever marry him now. With a sigh, she switched off the light and slowly made her way outside to the car.

CHAPTER TEN

'WELL, I give up,' Peggy said in an exasperated tone. 'First Peter, now Alex. What does it take to keep you engaged to a man?'

Jennie smiled at her friend. 'Well, Peter was hardly my fault, and with Alex it just didn't work out.'

It was two days after her hasty departure from Alex's, and they were sitting at the table in her own kitchen drinking coffee. Jennie had no intention of telling Peggy exactly why she had broken her engagement with Alex. That was a secret she would carry with her to the grave. Cold chills still ran up and down her spine whenever she thought about it.

'Well,' Peggy was demanding sternly, 'what do you intend to do with yourself now?'

'Oh, Peggy,' she said with a sigh. 'To tell you the truth, I hardly know where to begin. I might as well stay here for a while, at least until I get the house back in shape. You can see for yourself what a mess those rotten tenants left it in. I called Mr Simms the other morning to tell him to take the house off the market. He recommended a good cleaning service, and I'm going to call them today to arrange an appointment.'

Peggy cut herself another slice of coffee cake. 'Sounds to me as though you've got things pretty much under control. Very efficient, I'd say.'

Jennie made a face. 'Yes, but I still have to think about finding a job. Dad left me the house and a little money, but it won't support me forever.'

'Do you have a line on anything?'

'I thought first I'd call Dr Watkins, Dad's old part-ner. He offered me a job after Dad died. Maybe he can at least give me some temporary work just to tide me over. Then later on I'll look into the possibility of getting training for a more permanent job.'

Peggy raised her eyebrows. 'You? A career girl? I never thought I'd see the day!'

Jennie got up and went to the stove for the pot of coffee. 'Well, it looks as though I might be stuck with it, whether I like it or not,' she said drily. She refilled their cups and sat back down. 'Especially now that I have only myself to rely on. With two broken romances behind me, I'm beginning to think fate doesn't have a mate in store for me.'

'Oh, that's silly!' Peggy exclaimed. 'Look at me! I've wanted a career since we graduated from high school five years ago, but I'm still keeping an eye out for my own great romance.' She gave Jennie a wistful look. 'I don't suppose now that you and Alex have called it off he might. . .' She made a face and shook her head sadly. 'No,' she said with a sigh. 'I don't think I'm his type.'

Jennie didn't say anything. In the two days she'd been back in her old home she hadn't heard a word from him. For all she knew, he could have driven his car off a cliff the night he went storming out of the house after attacking her. Or, what was more likely, gone after Pamela.

Every time the telephone rang, she'd steeled herself, dreading having to speak to him again, but he was obviously just as determined as she was to remain stonily silent.

'Have you seen Peter lately?' Peggy was asking her now.

'No,' Jennie replied in surprise. 'Of course not. Why should I see him?'

'Well, he's coming up the path right now.' Peggy rose to her feet and drained her coffee. 'Time for me to get back to work, anyway. Thanks for the lunch.'

She grabbed her handbag and made a hasty exit. Jennie trailed along after her as far as the front door. What in the world did Peter want? She hadn't seen him or heard anything about him since that day he'd shown up at the ranch, nor had she expected to. Their whole relationship was a thing of the past.

When Peggy opened the door, he was standing on the other side already, his hand raised in the air to knock.

'Hi, Peter,' Peggy said lightly. 'How's the doctor business?'

'Not bad,' Peter said with a dubious smile.

She breezed past him and called over her shoulder to Jennie, 'Thanks for the coffee. I'll talk to you later.'

When she'd gone, Jennie turned and glanced at Peter, who was still just standing there on the front porch, watching Peggy as she disappeared from view.

'Well, what brings you here, Peter?' she asked coolly.

He gave her a rather hangdog look. 'Oh, I have a week off and decided to come up here and visit my parents.' He shifted his feet awkwardly on the porch. 'Er, Jennie, could I come in for a minute? I'd like to talk to you.'

'I don't know, Peter. I have an awful lot to do.'

'Please. It won't take long.'

'Oh, all right. But just for a minute. I think there's still some coffee left.'

He followed her down the hall to the kitchen and sat down in the chair Peggy had just vacated, staring out of the window at the garden. It was a fine day in early March, with bright sunshine cutting a swath across the green lawn through the jacaranda trees.

When Jennie had poured his coffee and sat down across from him, he turned to her and said a little wistfully, 'There are a lot of memories in this house, aren't there, Jennie?'

'I suppose so,' she said carefully. She glanced at her watch. 'Listen, Peter——' she began.

'I know. I'll get straight to the point.' He took a quick swallow of coffee, then took a deep breath and gave her a direct look. 'The long and short of it is, Jennie, that my engagement is off.'

Jennie stared. 'You mean you and Sheila?' He nodded. 'That's too bad,' she went on. 'She seemed— er—I mean, she was very beautiful.'

Peter shrugged non-committally. 'I guess. Too bad it was only on the surface.' The undertone of bitterness in his voice was unmistakable.

'Well, I am sorry. But these things happen, don't they?'

He reddened at the oblique reference to their own past history, and there was a short silence while he finished his coffee. Jennie couldn't help the fleeting glow of satisfaction she felt at his news. It was hard to feel really sorry for his disappointment when he had treated her so badly. Now, however, she just wanted him to leave so that she could get on with her chores.

'Well, Peter,' she said, and started to rise from her chair.

'Wait,' he said. 'Just one more thing.'

She sat back down and waited impatiently. He frowned down at his empty coffee-cup for a few moments, making circles with it on the table-top. Then he cleared his throat and gave her another direct look.

'I want you to know how glad I was to hear that you'd left Alex Knight's ranch, quit your job there.' He paused for a moment, waiting, but she kept quiet. 'There was a rumour that you two were engaged to be married,' he faltered on. Still she remained silent. 'I couldn't really believe that,' he said in a firmer tone.

She raised an eyebrow at him. 'Oh? Why not?'

'Well, for one thing, he's too old for you.'

'I don't call thirty-seven old,' she rejoined tartly.

'Maybe not. But, aside from that, he's just not your type.'

'And what is my type, Peter?' she said.

She was growing angry with him now. Just because his little romance hadn't worked out was no reason for him to come back here taking cheap shots at Alex.

And why on earth was she defending *that* monster? Men! she thought disgustedly. The whole lot of them made her sick.

She rose abruptly to her feet. 'Listen, Peter, I don't want to discuss my personal life with you. And I really do have a lot of things to do today. So, if you don't mind. . .'

He rose slowly to his feet. 'All right, Jennie. I guess there's no point in beating about the bush. I'll get straight to the real reason I'm here. In fact, it's why I came out to see you at Alex's place before.' He squared his shoulders and looked directly into her eyes. 'The truth of it is, Jennie, I still want to marry you, if you'll have me.'

She goggled at him in sheer disbelief. If he had told her that he had decided to give up his medical career and enter a monastery, she couldn't have been more shocked. It was the last thing in the world she had expected, and she didn't know whether to laugh or cry or kick him—or kiss him.

He gave her a pathetic look. 'The thing is, I never really did stop loving you. I guess I was just a small-town boy who got carried away by Sheila and her big-city sophistication.' He shrugged diffidently. 'You know, the bright lights in the fast lane. Then when her father offered me that plummy residency, and she seemed so interested in me. . .'

While he spoke, Jennie's mind raced. Here was Peter, the great love of her life, offering himself to her on a plate. Did she want him? Did she still love him? In one way, it would solve everything. Marriage to a rising young doctor would give her exactly what she'd always wanted—a home, security, a family. There would be no need to find a job or train for a career.

She was tempted, strongly tempted. She examined him carefully. It was the same old Peter. Nothing had really changed. Still, she had to know.

'And now she's thrown you over?' she asked.

He shook his head vigorously. 'No. It wasn't like that. I never really loved her. It just took me a while to realise it. Then, when I started hearing rumours about you and Alex Knight, it suddenly dawned on me that you were what I really wanted all along.'

'I don't know, Peter,' she said slowly. 'You really hurt me, you know. I don't think I can forget that so easily.'

'I can understand that,' he said eagerly. 'All I want you to do is think about it. I'll be around for the rest of the week. Maybe we could go out to dinner, take in a movie?' He grinned boyishly. 'Just like old times.'

He moved a step closer to her and reached out a hand, but she backed away quickly. She wasn't ready for that. She was still stunned by his unexpected proposal and needed time to consider what it was that she really wanted.

'We'll see,' she said. 'Give me a day or two to think about it.'

He dropped his hand. 'OK. I can understand that. There's no hurry. Today is Saturday. Let's say I give you a call on Wednesday afternoon. Then we can take it from there.'

When he had gone, Jennie sat at the table in the kitchen by herself for a long time, going over their conversation step by step. There was no doubt in her mind that he'd been sincere. And she did still care about him. Perhaps not with the old uncritical adoration, but there was still a genuine affection.

Why not? The only thing really holding her back was her pride. She didn't need to decide today, anyway. She had enough on her mind just to get the house in order. Then, when he called on Wednesday, she would see how she felt and try to have an answer for him.

It wasn't until she'd gone to the telephone to dial the cleaning service that the thought of Alex popped into her head. How could she ever have thought that she was in love with two men who were as unlike each other as night and day? Although both of them had hurt her, it was in entirely different ways.

She wasn't afraid of Peter the way she was of Alex. Peter had behaved childishly, like a spoilt little boy reaching out and grabbing what he wanted no matter who got hurt. Alex, on the other hand, had treated her badly, to be sure, but as a grown man, not a child—a man whom she had aroused by her own actions.

And had Alex really harmed her? She thought back to all the years he'd come to the house as her father's friend. He'd always been so gentle with her, so kind. Until that night. But hadn't that been partly her fault? She had provoked him then, challenged him, practically forced him into betraying emotions he'd always managed to keep hidden before. But when things had got out of hand and she'd become frightened, he'd still had the maturity and self-control to stop.

There was no point in thinking about that, she decided as she dialled. With Peter she would be safe. Alex Knight was out of her life for good.

By Wednesday, Jennie had almost made up her mind to accept Peter's proposal. After all, it was what she'd always planned to do, marry Peter. The past several months without him were already fading from her mind. They weren't important.

The cleaners had come the day before, and the house was now back in its old order. She wondered if Peter would want to come back to Santa Lucia to practise now that her father was gone, or if he intended to stay with the hospital in San Francisco. If he did want to come back, she would like to live here in her old home.

They had so much to talk about, so many things to decide. When he called her later that afternoon, she would invite him here for dinner. Then they could make more definite plans.

But first she had some unfinished business. Several of her belongings were still out at Alex's. She'd been hoping that he might pack them up and deliver them to her, but she still hadn't heard a word from him. He could have moved from the house, he could even have *died*, and she wouldn't know it.

She would just have to go out there and get them herself. If she was going to agree to Peter's proposal tonight, she wanted to start out on a clean slate.

Half an hour later, she was in the car on her way out into the country. She hadn't bothered to call him to tell him that she was coming. He would be out in the vineyard or at the winery, anyway, and with luck she could get her things packed up and leave without his even knowing she was there at all.

When she arrived, his station-wagon was in its usual spot in the driveway. She parked beside it, and had a quick look around. There was no sign of him. Although it was warm, the sky had clouded over that morning, and as she hurried towards the shelter of the porch drops of rain spattered down on her face.

The front door was unlocked, as usual, and she made straight for her old bedroom. It was exactly as she had left it; even her ruined clothing was still lying in a heap on the floor where she had dropped it after tearing it off that night.

She worked swiftly and efficiently, anxious to finish and get out of there in case Alex decided to come back to the house early. Outside the rain had begun to pour down in earnest, with sharp gusts of wind slashing heavy drops against the bedroom window. Not a very good day for working in the fields, but there was always plenty to do inside at the winery.

In under half an hour she had collected everything into two suitcases and three cardboard boxes. It took her four trips out to the car to get it all stowed away.

By the time she had made three of them, she was soaked to the skin and cursing herself for not thinking to bring rain gear.

Finally, she picked up the last load, the heaviest box of them all, containing books and records. With a sigh of relief, she nudged the bedroom door shut with her hips, then started trudging down the hall to the front door.

It opened just as she got there, and Alex walked inside. He took one look at her, then came towards her, reaching out to take the box from her.

'Here,' he said, lifting it out of her arms. 'Let me do that.'

Her first impulse was to refuse his help, but there was no point in arguing about such a small thing. 'All right,' she said coolly. 'Thank you.' She relinquished the heavy box and started to walk past him.

However, he gave no sign of moving. Instead, after simply standing there staring at her for a long moment, he kicked the door shut and set the box down on the floor.

'I could have done this for you if you'd let me know you were coming,' he said quietly. 'In fact, if I hadn't just happened to see your car out in the driveway I wouldn't even have known you were here.'

'That was my intention,' she said stiffly. 'I thought it would be best if we didn't meet again.'

'I see. Well, I won't keep you, but I would like just a few minutes of your time. I want to apologise for what happened the other night.'

'There's no need for that. It's over. I'd rather not discuss it at all.'

'I can't say I blame you. I behaved abominably. I'm not going to give you any trumped-up explanations or try to make excuses, if that's what's worrying you. My only real concern is your welfare. I know I frightened you, and I would never forgive myself if I thought I'd done you any lasting harm. If only for the sake of my friendship with your father, I'd like to try to make it up to you in some way if I can.'

Each word he uttered only fed her resentment, until by the time he was through she was beside herself with fury. How could he stand there and speak so calmly to her after what had passed between them? Less than a week ago he'd been making passionate love to her. Now he might have been explaining to a customer why a particular vintage was not quite up to par.

What she wanted, with all her heart, was to hurt him in some way, to pierce beyond that polite, distant façade, to see real pain in those cool grey eyes.

'That's very noble of you,' she said in a mocking tone, 'but you can forget it. There's nothing you can do for me now except leave me alone.'

When he simply continued to gaze steadily at her, without uttering another word, her anger finally spilled over. She couldn't speak. She actually started to raise a hand to him, as though to strike him or claw her fingernails down his cheek, ripping the skin, drawing blood.

Finally he spoke. 'All right,' he said in a tight voice. 'If that's what you want.'

It was then that she found her tongue. 'Well, what did you expect?' she shouted. 'First you treat me like a little girl, barely old enough to wipe her own nose, much less be treated like a real live flesh-and-blood woman. Then, when it finally dawns on you that I'm not a child, you almost rape me!'

At her words, his head jerked back as though she

had indeed hit him, and she saw that she had struck a nerve at last. Folding her arms in front of her, she gazed with intense satisfaction at the deep red flush that covered his face, the pain that darkened the grey of his eyes to a deep, wintry slate colour, the frown that creased his forehead.

'You were never in the least danger of that,' he said in a low voice, 'and you know it.'

'I *didn't* know it!' she cried.

He gave her a direct, challenging look. 'All right. Have it your way. I was all prepared to take full responsibility for what happened, and to try to make it up to you in any way I could.' His features hardened and he took a step towards her. 'I'm not trying to make excuses for myself, but on some level, and for heaven knows what reason, you deliberately provoked me.'

She squared her shoulders and lifted her chin. 'If I did, it was only to get some evidence that you had any feelings for me at all, and no amount of provocation could ever justify the way you used your superior physical strength against me. However,' she went on loftily, 'I'm not going to stand here and argue with you about that. It doesn't matter now.' She gave him a defiant look. 'I've decided to marry Peter Fleming, after all.'

He gave her one horrified look of disbelief. 'No!' he shot out. 'You can't do that!'

She saw immediately that she had wounded him deeply, and with a heady sense of triumph, pressed on. 'Why not? Surely, you don't think I'd marry *you* now?'

'No, I don't,' he bit back. 'Not for a minute. I see now that that was only a pipe-dream of mine. I should never have considered it in the first place. But not

Fleming. I can't bear to see you throw yourself away on such a shallow man.'

Jennie's mouth dropped open at this impassioned speech, and her moment of triumph quickly faded. It wasn't at all what she had expected. She had wanted to hurt him, to spark his jealousy by telling him she was giving herself to another man. But he didn't seem to be in the least jealous of Peter!

In fact, he actually seemed to be saying that Peter wasn't good enough for her, but without offering himself as a replacement. Was it possible that all he really cared about was her welfare?

She searched his face for an answer, and all she saw there was the dark shadow of pain. She had seen that look before, and her heart had gone out to him. Now she had put it there herself.

Suddenly, hot tears stung behind her eyes. In spite of everything, she still loved him, still wanted him, still longed for his touch. But could she trust him? Although it was true that she had intentionally prodded him into a display of passion that night, he was the one who had lost control.

She stood there, her head whirling crazily with conflicting emotion. Only one thing seemed certain. She couldn't leave him like this. She had to make him understand.

As she searched her heart for the right words, the tears began to spill over. With a noisy, gulping cry, she put her face in her hands and broke out into uncontrollable sobs.

Immediately, Alex was at her side, his arms around her, holding her close, stroking her hair. 'Don't cry, Jennie,' he murmured soothingly into her ear. 'Come on, now.'

'Oh, Alex,' she wailed against his chest. 'I don't want to marry Peter.'

He put a hand under her chin and tilted her head up. With a loud sniffle, she raised her face to his and gazed up into the fathomless depths of his smoky-grey eyes. Soberly, he reached in his trouser-pocket, took out a clean handkerchief and began to wipe the tears from her face.

'What do you want then, Jennie?' he asked gently. His hands moved to her shoulders, gripping her hard. 'Oh, if I could only undo what happened!' He smiled bleakly. 'The saddest words, right? What might have been.' He stared down into her eyes. 'I'd give anything I possess to make it up to you, Jennie. Anything. If I thought there was the faintest chance you might——' He broke off and looked away.

Hope rose within her like a burning flame. 'Alex, I think it's time for a little truth-telling here.' She took a deep breath. 'I did provoke you the other night, but the reason I did was that I couldn't face marrying you without some evidence that you cared for me, that you desired me, that you felt something for me beyond a paternal affection.'

His dark eyebrows shot up. 'How could you ever have doubted that?'

'Well, what did you ever do to make me believe otherwise? Aside from one or two brief episodes, the most I ever got from you in the way of real feeling was a pat on the head for being a good little girl.'

'All right,' he said with a firm nod. 'I guess I have to admit that I perpetuated that myth myself. I suppose I had to treat you like a little girl because, if I once allowed myself to think of you as the woman you actually are, I was afraid of what I might do. Then when you accused me of treating Pamela with more passion than I'd ever shown for you, all the pent-up desire I've felt all these years just spilled over and I went a little mad.'

'Yes,' she agreed firmly. 'You did.'

He spread his arms helplessly. 'But whatever the cost, whatever you decide to do, I've got to make it clear to you how I feel, even if it's too late and I've destroyed any feeling you might have had for me by my inexcusable behaviour. All I can say is that I hope you'll forgive me in time, and, no matter what you decide, I swear to you that it will never happen again.'

As she looked up at him and saw the depth of emotion shining out of his face, she believed that he meant every word, that she would never have anything to fear from him again.

'Yes, Alex,' she said at last. 'I do forgive you.'

He breathed a deep sigh of relief. 'Thank heaven for that, anyway. And you're not going to throw yourself away on Fleming, are you? Please, don't do that.' He hesitated, reddening. 'Perhaps in time, as you learn to trust me again, we might even be able to start over, this time without any lying or evasions.'

'What—what are you saying, Alex?' she faltered.

'I'm saying that I love you, Jennie. I'm through hiding it from you or myself. You're right. It's time— way past time—for absolute honesty between us.'

As their eyes met, Jennie knew in the depths of her heart that he was telling her the real truth at last, and that he meant every word. This man was the one she loved, had always loved, with her whole being, and all thoughts of Peter flew out of her mind. Still, she had to be certain.

'Oh, Alex,' she said, 'is it really me you want, a grown woman, and not my father's little girl?'

'My darling girl,' he said soberly, 'you're a lot of things, some of them quite aggravating, but the one thing I'll never do again is think of you as a child.' He raised a quizzical eyebrow. 'As a matter of fact, you're definitely all woman, from the top of your head to the tips of your toes.'

'All right,' she said softly. 'If you're sure. . .'

A bright light of hope suddenly glittered in his eyes, and the corners of his mouth quirked up. 'I'll show you,' he said softly.

His strong arms came around her then, and his mouth covered hers, softly and tentatively at first, giving her time to draw back, then gradually deepening into a long, passionate kiss that seemed to draw her very soul out of her. This time there was no urgency, yet no holding back, only a slow, seductive warmth that built up gradually until finally, with a low groan, he drew his mouth from hers and gazed down at her.

'I want you,' he said, his low voice throbbing with emotion. 'All of you. Body and soul, mine forever, in every way possible. I want to love you, to take care of you.' Dropping his eyes, he reached out one hand to place it on her heaving breast. 'And I want you to meet my desire, my need for you, to be my wife, to give me children.'

As the hand on her breast began to move in slow circles, their eyes locked together and Jennie's whole body became flooded with a delicious warmth. Swaying on her feet, she pressed herself up against him. His hard need for her was clearly evident, and she gave herself up to the ecstasy of the moment completely.

'How about it, Jennie?' he asked. 'Will you let me

take care of you? Will you marry me? Will you be my love?'

'Oh, Alex!' she cried, throwing her arms around his neck. 'I've always loved you. I know that now. I just didn't recognise it for what it really was.'

'And no more nonsense about marrying Fleming?'

She almost had to laugh as she compared them mentally, the man and the boy. Peter had never come close to arousing this kind of passionate response in her, this intensity of longing to become one with another human being.

She shook her head. 'No,' she said happily. 'That's all over. Peter was only a habit.'

He nodded and gave her a smile of intense satisfaction. Then slowly, deliberately, he reached down and undid the top button of her blouse. Jennie held her breath, all her senses alert. He stopped then before going on, his hand at her throat, and gave her a questioning look.

Searching her mind for a way to answer that question, she raised her hands and put them flat against his heaving chest, where she could feel his heart thudding heavily under her touch.

'Yes,' she whispered. 'I love you, Alex. I want you.'

She closed her eyes then and allowed her head to fall back, as his fingers lingered over each button to run lightly over every inch of bare skin as it was revealed. When he was through, he drew aside the folds of her blouse and lowered his head to place hot kisses on her face, her throat, her bare breasts, running his hands over her ribs, her waist, and down underneath the waistband of her skirt.

Then, in a sudden swift movement, he picked her up and, with her arms twined around his neck, carried her to his own bedroom. He kicked the door open and laid her gently on top of the bed. He stood gazing down at her for several moments, his eyes alight with desire, then slowly began to strip off his own clothing.

As she watched him, the tanned, lithe body gradually revealed, the broad, muscular chest with its old scar, the narrow hips, the long legs covered with silky black hair, she suddenly realised that this very room was the scene of their last painful encounter.

Only this time it would be different, she thought as the hard body settled down next to her and she was gathered into his strong protective arms once again. This time she would be an active participant, not a passive victim. She'd found the right man at last, and she intended to keep him.

SOLITAIRE – Lisa Gregory   £3.50

Emptiness and heartache lay behind the facade of Jennifer Taylor's glittering Hollywood career. Bitter betrayal had driven her to become a successful actress, but now at the top, where else could she go?

SWEET SUMMER HEAT – Katherine Burton   £2.99

Rebecca Whitney has a great future ahead of her until a sultry encounter with a former lover leaves her devastated...

THE LIGHT FANTASTIC – Peggy Nicholson   £2.99

In this debut novel, Peggy Nicholson focuses on her own profession... Award-winning author Tripp Wetherby's fear of flying could ruin the promotional tour for his latest blockbuster. Rennie Markell is employed to cure his phobia, whatever it takes!

These three new titles will be out in bookshops from February 1990.

W🌐RLDWIDE

2 NEW TITLES FOR JANUARY 1990

Mariah by Sandra Canfield is the first novel in a sensational quartet of sisters in search of love… Mariah's sensual and provocative behaviour contrasts enigmatically with her innocent and naive appearance… Only the maverick preacher can recognise her true character and show her the way to independence and true love.

£2.99

Faye is determined to make a success of the farm she has inherited – but she hadn't accounted for the bitter battle with neighbour, Seth Carradine, who was after the land himself. In desperation she turns to him for help, and an interesting bargain is struck. **Kentucky Woman** by Casey Douglas, best-selling author of Season of Enchantment. **£2.99**

W❂RLDWIDE

TASTY FOOD COMPETITION!

How would you like a years supply of Mills & Boon Romances ABSOLUTELY FREE? Well, you can win them! All you have to do is complete the word puzzle below and send it in to us by March. 31st. 1990. The first 5 correct entries picked out of the bag after that date will win **a years supply of Mills & Boon Romances** (*ten books every month - worth £162*) What could be easier?

```
H O L L A N D A I S E R
E Y E G G O W H A O H A R
R S E E C L A I R U C T T
B T K K A E T S I F I A A
E E T I S M A L C F U T T
U R C M T L H E E L Q O U
G S I U T F O N O E D U I
N H L S O T O N E F M I
I S R S O M A C W A A L
R I A E E T I R J A E L
E F G L L P T O T V R E
M O U S S E E O D O C P
```

CLAM	HOLLANDAISE	OYSTERS	SPICE
COD	JAM	PRAWN	STEAK
CREAM	LEEK	QUICHE	TART
ECLAIR	LEMON	RATATOUILLE	
EGG	MELON	RICE	
FISH	MERINGUE	RISOTTO	
GARLIC	MOUSSE	SALT	
HERB	MUSSELS	SOUFFLE	

PLEASE TURN OVER FOR DETAILS ON HOW TO ENTER

HOW TO ENTER

All the words listed overleaf, below the word puzzle, are hidden in the grid. You can find them by reading the letters forward, backwards, up or down, or diagonally. When you find a word, circle it or put a line through it, the remaining letters (which you can read from left to right, from the top of the puzzle through to the bottom) will ask a romantic question.

After you have filled in all the words, don't forget to fill in your name and address in the space provided and pop this page in an envelope (you don't need a stamp) and post it today. Hurry - competition ends March 31st 1990.

Mills & Boon Competition,
FREEPOST,
P.O. Box 236,
Croydon,
Surrey. CR9 9EL

Only one entry per household

Hidden Question _____

_____

Name _____

Address _____

_____

_____

_____ Postcode _____

mps
MAILING
PREFERENCE
SERVICE

COMP 8